Trino's Choice

Diane Gonzales Bertrand

PIÑATA
BOOKS

PIÑATA BOOKS
ARTE PÚBLICO PRESS
HOUSTON, TEXAS
1999

This volume is made possible through grants from the National Endowment for the Arts (a federal agency), Andrew W. Mellon Foundation, the Lila Wallace-Reader's Digest Fund and the City of Houston through The Cultural Arts Council of Houston, Harris County.

Piñata Books are full of surprises!

Piñata Books

An imprint of
Arte Público Press
University of Houston
Houston, Texas 77204-2174

Cover illustration and design by Vega Design Group

Bertrand, Diane Gonzales.
    Trino's Choice / Diane Gonzales Bertrand.
    p.   cm.
    Summary: Frustrated by his poor financial situation and hoping to impress a smart girl, seventh grader Trino falls in with a bad crowd led by an older teen with a vicious streak.
    ISBN 1-55885-279-4.—ISBN 1-55885-268-9 (pbk. : alk. paper)
    [1. Crime — Fiction.   2. Mexican Americans — Fiction.]
I. Title.
PZ7.B46357Tr   1999
[Fic]—dc21   98-56132
                                                              CIP

0 1 2 3 4 5 6 7 8   10 9 8 7 6 5 4 3 2

To
Trinidad Sanchez, Jr.
for his inspiration and encouragement

For
the middle school students
and their teachers
who asked me to write a book for them

Thank you.

Chapter One
Trino

Trino had to run or die. Hands clenched into fists, he ran through the hot dust that stuck to his tongue and made his eyes burn.

He cut through the alley behind the old Texaco; he didn't stop to read the new tags from the local gangs that grunged up the back walls. Tall brown weeds whipped against his jeans as his open blue shirt flapped behind him like a sheet on the clothesline.

Then he heard the whistle and knew they weren't far behind.

He cursed his stupidity for running this way. Just fields and the highway ahead. They'd check the Texaco first, then find him panting like a dog in the middle of the field.

This was no good. Trino saw buildings to his left in the distance: A line of brown adobe buildings with rows of dry straw as a roof. He ran towards them though he knew they were only pitiful shops for tourists who thought South Texas coyotes wore bandanas and everybody had a barbed-wire cactus in his front yard. A few cars were parked in the gravel lot, but nobody was walking around.

He wondered where to hide. *NELIDA'S* looked like a woman's shop. As soon as he'd go in, the owner would give him the *ojo*. *SOCORRO BAZAAR* sounded like a place to buy a cement *burro* or ugly *piñatas*. What for?

FITO'S TACOS made him hungry, but it was a lousy

1

place for hiding. The place on the corner was a shop called
THE BOOK BASKET.

He slowed as he neared the porch. The porch boards
were warped and there was a bunch of tourist junk on the
walls, but it looked like it might be air-conditioned.

The door handle stuck into his hand as he pushed it
down. It didn't budge, so he pushed his shoulder into the
red door and got it open.

He blinked at the darkness, a big difference from the
sunshine he had been running through. There wasn't
much light to see with—only a string of red jalapeño light-
bulbs running around this room, small like a closet.

Quickly he glanced over the shelves on the back wall.
Certain books were leaning against the wall, their front
covers facing him. He saw some T-shirts on a rack to his
left, and then he spotted the square cash register sitting on
a L-shaped counter that hooked into a glass case that held
clay pots and tourquoise jewelry.

The place looked empty, or else the owner was in the
back some place.

Was there enough time to hit the cash? He could get
something out of this rotten day after all.

Trino had only taken one step towards the counter
when he heard, "Hi, can I help you?"

A short colorless figure suddenly appeared and faced
him down.

Trino realized it was a white lady, with messy, light
hair and fat cheeks. She was wearing something gray, shirt
and pants, and it wasn't until she stepped closer that he
smelled the faint odor of flowers.

"Got a lot of books here. What kind you looking for?"
She moved herself between him and the cash register, and
because Trino was her height, she could stare him in the
eye.

He didn't blink, but his mind was whizzing. *Was she*

alone here? Could he shove her down and get the money and be out before the guys showed up? Maybe he could buy his way out of the mess he was in.

"Hey, I know you," the lady said, moving her face even closer.

Trino felt a fire boiling in his stomach and got control of his head. He wanted to get out of this place. Fast. He stepped back, ready to run out, but the lady locked a finger onto his shirt pocket.

"You're one of those kids who's doing a book report on Rivera's book, right? I just got some copies in yesterday. Come on." She turned to go some place, tugging him along. "I was in the back, eating my lunch. Stick around. I'll show you where the books are."

Trino should have called her something and left, but when the lady pulled him, he realized there was another room where the air was cooler. She was taking him into it. Hiding here wouldn't be too bad, even if he had to fake it—like *he* had to do a book report. She seemed dumb enough to believe somebody like him would even *care* about a book.

Down a lumpy ramp, she led him into a second room. Two uncovered bulbs hung from the wooden slats under the straw ceiling. He saw shelves of books around the walls and corner tables with books laid out. They had colored shiny covers and bright pictures.

Kids' books for teachers, he figured. Books he could never take home from school when he was a kid because his little brothers would tear up the pages and then the teachers would yell at him. More trouble he didn't need.

The next room was bigger, and it had long skinny flourescent bulbs above that gave lots of light, and also showed how many books could get stuffed into one place. Bookshelves were all over the walls. Books jammed together like wooden fences. There were books in boxes, their spines facing up so he could see the titles. Books were lined into plastic milk crates, and more were in some wooden crates that had pictures of grapefruits painted on them. Books were stuck into tall metal racks that spun around. There was even a shopping basket with no wheels that books were piled into.

Two scratched-up wooden chairs with straw seats stood next to a flowery blue table in one corner. The table had a few books tossed on it, as if somebody had looked through them, but decided not to waste the money after all.

"I got the book you need on the second shelf over," the lady said, gesturing with a white hand that bore no jewelry. "Look around. I'll be back."

She left Trino standing in the middle of the room. It was the best place he could have chosen to hide, and he could only laugh. He wondered if there was anything better than books in this place and started snooping. He found a pair of red vinyl beanbags behind the shopping cart, and dragged them into a spot behind the racks. If he sat in the corner, pretending to read a book, maybe the *gringa* would leave him alone. It was cool here, easy to fall asleep.

"Hey!" came a voice from behind him.

Trino kicked the bags and turned around, fists clenched.

"I sometimes kick them a little to get them comfortable too."

Trino felt both mad and stupid. The white lady had just scared the spit out of him, but now she stood holding a can of red soda and an egg. She extended her hands towards him. "Can't offer you much, but I don't mind sharing."

His eyebrows pressed down into his nose. "No," he growled, then after a pause, said, "No . . . thanks."

"Can't enjoy a good book without a snack. Granny Wagner taught me that." Her squinty eyes widened into blue circles. "Take the food and tell me later what you think of the book."

She lowered her hand as if she would drop the egg into his lap if he didn't take it, so he grabbed onto the hard, cold egg and the icy soda. He liked the cool, wet feel of them, especially with his mouth still tasting dust and his stomach empty since last night.

Scratching her fuzzy reddish head, the lady wandered back into another room.

Trino flopped himself into the beanbags and relaxed. He opened up the soda and took a long swig of it. The soda seemed to sting his throat as it rinsed out the dusty fear that had brought him to this place.

He found a narrow hole between the wall and the floor that was a great place to drop the pieces of eggshell as he unpeeled the hard-boiled egg. He was munching down the egg, looking up and behind him, when he noticed the cracks of sunlight in the form of a rectangle. He realized he was sitting in front of a door, or a spot of the wall that used to be a door. He raised his fingers to a nearby crack and felt the hot air press into his skin. A shiver slid down his back, and he washed it away with another long drink of soda.

With nothing else to do, Trino's eyes started to focus in on the titles of the books lined up at his level. He grabbed one from the shelf and looked at the front cover. There was a picture of a black bird carrying a rosary in its beak.

The author's name was Morelos, like his uncle's. Trino opened up a page in the middle and started reading about a *curandero*, a healer who cured a village of evil spirits. Trino couldn't pronounce some of the words, but he liked the suspense. He understood why the town could be so scared of the evil sign that had appeared on mountain top.

Trino's heart shook with excitement as he read through the description of how the *curandero* mixed potions and chanted prayers. The emotions of the characters grew intense. Even the ground under Trino seemed to tremble as an evil spirit tried to hold fast to its claim.

Angry voices on the other side of the wall sent the evil spirit flying right into Trino's backbone. He sat up, tossing the book aside. Up on one knee he peeked through one of the cracks.

He saw little more than legs, pairs of faded jeans, and dirty shoes.

"Could he have gone inside here?"

"What, for a book?"

"Books and a crazy old lady? Valdo says the place is like a coffin inside."

"Still, we should check it out."

Trino hunched down, just in case the guys could some-how peek in. He felt a cold sweat at the back of his neck. He looked around nervously, wishing for something he could use as a weapon. *Books! Worthless books!*

"I found this biography of Rivera—did you lose some-thing?" The lady had reappeared with a fat brown book in her hands.

Trino wished he could take that book and slap it against Rosca's rat face right now. Only Rosca was on the other side of the wall, and Trino was right here with this crazy Book Lady, scared to say anything that might be heard through the cracks in the wall. Quickly, he shook his head. Trino hunched his shoulders together, feeling like a dumb dog in the street, just waiting to get hit by a car.

"Oh—okay," she said, then opened up the book. "I thought if you needed some background on Rivera for your book report, you could read something out of this. Teachers like this kind of stuff, you know. Always good for extra credit. Extra credit always help for report cards, right?"

Her words gave him a headache, but his own words could get him killed. So Trino nodded again and just pulled the book from her hands. He didn't look into her face at all and definitely wanted to avoid those eyes of her, so blue and sharp they could probably slit tires.

Wanting to get away from the cracks in the wall where the guys might still be, Trino carried the book to the straw chair and flowered table and sat there instead.

He had just set his eyes upon the cover—a picture of a some guy named Tomás Rivera—when he heard boys' voices in the other room.

Book Lady, he thought, we're both in deep trouble now.

Chapter Two
School-Types

Every muscle in Trino's body tightened as he looked beyond the Book Lady to the group entering the room.

When they came into the light, though, Trino realized it wasn't Rosca and his gang. It was only three boys and a couple of girls. They all talked at the same time, greeting the Book Lady as if she was someone they all knew.

"So are we too early, or too late, or what?" one boy asked her.

"You're a day off. Emilce comes tomorrow," the Book Lady said.

A girl with a red shirt slugged the boy in the shoulder. "I *told* you, Jimmy. I said the poetry man was coming on Saturday."

"No harm done. You can all come back again," the Book Lady said, and then looked back at Trino. "Can you come tomorrow too?"

Now all the kids were staring at him. He could have given them the *ojo*, but decided not to blow his school-boy story with the Book Lady. He passed his eyes over theirs like when he was just looking but not buying. He shrugged his shoulders together.

"Who's this, Maggie?" asked a nice-looking girl with thick black hair. She wore it loose and wavy over her shoulders.

The Book Lady's hand dropped on Trino's back. "He's doing a book report on one of Rivera's books. Name's—

uh, what did you tell me? Sorry."

"They call me Trino," he said, and couldn't take his eyes off the girl with the black hair. What was *her* name?

The girl gave him a little smile, then turned to look at the books in the shopping cart. "I might buy a book tomorrow. Have anything interesting, Maggie?"

"Everything in that basket's interesting, hon," the Book Lady said, as she joined the girl at the cart, and started rattling on about books like a librarian.

"You go to Carson, man?" the boy called Jimmy asked Trino.

Trino barely nodded his head. He had seen them around, seventh-graders like himself. He knew their type okay. The kind teachers liked; answered questions, did their homework. Not the kids he'd choose for friends. Probably couldn't pick a lock or pound a soda machine until it paid off. He never had hassles from school-types, though—probably 'cause he never gave them any trouble.

As he stole another look at the girl moving around the books in the shopping cart, Trino wondered if maybe he should pretend a while longer and see what paid off.

Suddenly, a small hand brushed over Trino's shoulder, and fingernails painted like green bullets were pointing to the open book.

"He's the guy who wrote the book Miss Jimenez wants us to read."

Trino said nothing as the girl in the red shirt moved closer to him. He smelled peanut butter when she spoke again. "Do you have Miss Jimenez for class?"

Trino muttered "No," hoping she'd go away and leave him alone.

"Miss Jimenez wants us all to buy Rivera's book. She says he writes about problems in real life. She says even our parents should read his book." The girl talked on, like school-types usually did, but Trino tuned her out.

He had no parents who would ever read books. His dad was dead, and his mom worked two jobs, sometimes three. She had no time to read. The kids in the bookstore had life too easy. If they could only sit inside his house a while, they'd know more about real problems than any book could show them.

The girl finally walked off, probably tired of listening to herself. One boy had joined Maggie and the girls at the shopping cart. The other two guys were in another spot thumbing through some books. Trino could still feel their eyes on him, though. Had they spotted Rosca before they came in? Had they guessed that Trino was hiding out?

Even if Trino left when the school-types did, he knew Rosca would still jump him. School-types would just run home scared and leave Trino to die.

Then a perfumy smell pushed Trino's vision of his broken body out of his head. He looked up to see the girl with black hair drop a couple of books onto the table. She stood across the table from him, holding another book in her hand. She had small hands, no ugly nail polish, and a small silver ring with a black stone on one finger.

He saw the slim brown face with reddish lips, a small nose, and wide, brown eyes. Her eyes looked good, not gooped over with black stuff. She puffed out a little laugh when she caught him looking at her.

"Do you like to read?" She seemed to be teasing him.

"Sure," Trino lied, drumming on the book with his fingers.

"Me too," she answered, only this time there was no laugh behind her words. "I go to the library, but Maggie has better stuff here. It's worth it to wait and buy my own books."

Trino nodded because he didn't know what to answer. What was wrong with him, anyway? His tongue seemed to fill up his throat. He wanted to spit, but he sure couldn't do it now.

"I'm Lisana," the girl said. "Trino, right?"

He nodded again, and felt like he had a rubber neck. He swallowed something thick with a taste of egg, red soda, and books. Then he asked her, "You go to Carson?"

"Yes. I used to go to Grande. Carson is better."

"It's 'cause it's new. Grande is older than my *abuela*." Trino was glad when she smiled. He wasn't sure if her type even knew Spanish. In his neighborhood, Spanish and English words mixed together like mud and water. Pieces of two languages often got him into trouble with schoolwork, especially with the *gringo* teachers.

The two guys in the corner suddenly came over to the table. Trino wondered which one had his claim on Lisana. Trino's back and shoulders tightened as the boy called Jimmy narrowed his eyes. He studied Trino a moment, before he spoke to Lisana.

"If we're going to come back tomorrow, we'd better go home, Lisana." The boy Jimmy spoke his words carefully, as if there was a secret message stuck between them. "You know how Abby gets."

Lisana sighed. "Yeah, okay. We'd better go."

The Book Lady brought the girl in the red shirt and the other boy up to the table as she came to join them. "Did you decide on anything, Lisana?"

"Maybe I'll buy the poetry book tomorrow, Maggie."

Trino waited for the Book Lady to get red-faced or make a growl like the old man at the corner store who got mad when Trino would rub the watermelons or shake a box of cereal but not buy anything. The Book Lady just picked up the books on the table and said, "Emilce Montoya is going to be famous someday, and you can tell everyone that you bought a signed copy of his poetry book at this store."

"Think we could sell his autograph for big bucks like a

ballplayer's?" the boy next to Jimmy said.

"Think we could sell your brain to science, Albert?" Jimmy answered, and the other kids laughed. Even Trino smiled.

Maggie looped her arm around Albert's shoulder. "Emilce will start reading at three. Don't be late 'cause you'll miss something special. I'm even going to have a bit to eat and drink too. Can't enjoy a good book without a snack."

Trino wondered if these kids liked cold eggs and red soda.

Lisana and Jimmy both promised the Book Lady they'd be back tomorrow for the poetry reading.

As Trino listened to them, he thought the school-types were crazy to want to listen to some man read poetry. Poetry was so dumb; stupid rhymes or broken sentences that made no sense. He'd rather get a slap on the head than try to figure out what some dumb poem meant.

The boys started heading out of the room with the Book Lady, but the girl in the red shirt hung back, tugging Lisana's arm to stay with her. She gave Trino a quick look in the eye, then dropped her gaze to the floor as she said in a quiet voice, "I need a copy of Rivera's book for English, Lisana. The library's all checked out, and Miss Jimenez wants us to get one by Monday. Will you buy it?"

"Don't you have any money?"

"Miss Jimenez says it's a great book. You can buy it and read it too. I'm just going to borrow it a few days. You're always buying books, Lisana. I need my money to buy something better."

Lisana's nose wrinkled up, as if she didn't like what the girl said. Then she pushed some air between her lips and shrugged. "I'll think about it, Janie." Her eyes looked up to catch Trino staring at her. She gave him a little wave. "See you tomorrow, Trino."

His body slid back into his chair, but he said nothing. The two girls rushed out after the boys.

Suddenly Trino straightened up like somebody popped him in the back. He needed to get out of here before the crazy Book Lady started in on him about reading books and listening to poetry.

He pushed the chair back and quickly moved to the side wall to peek through the cracks. There was no sign of Rosca or the guys, just the school-types leaving the shop in a group, heading back towards the road. Where was Rosca now? Did he go back to the park? Was he waiting behind this building? Trino fingered his throat, wishing he wore a silver medal to give him a little extra help from a *santo*.

He'd just have to head to the highway, and pray some neighbor going home from the blue jeans factory would give him a lift home before Rosca spotted him.

Trino's legs seemed wooden as he walked out of the book room, up the crooked ramp, and towards the little room in the front where people came into this place. When he saw the Book Lady at the counter, he felt a pinch inside his head. He still had to get past her.

She sprayed some stinky pine cleaner on the glass counter and wiped it up with a towel. "Emilce reads at three. Be here early so you can talk to him."

Trino merely stared, to let her know he wouldn't be back, but who could see his eyes in this dark place? He wondered how he got so stupid—being caught in a place that was worse than school. There was nothing here for him. He needed to get himself out the door and forget about today.

"Emilce's the best poet around, but no one notices. Last time his reading should have been on TV. It was that good," she said, still wiping off the counter.

The Book Lady kept talking, but Trino was already

inching back towards the door. The floor creaked under his feet, like some haunted house in a movie. Hopefully, he'd get out and home before this *bruja* cut out his liver and ate it for supper.

"Trino!" The Book Lady suddenly spoke in a loud voice.

Trino's hands clenched into fists. He knew whatever followed his name would be words he would fight.

"I want you back here tomorrow. You need to hear Emilce read."

Trino ground his teeth together. He hated to be ordered around. "I don't have to do what you say."

It was the first time he let himself be who he was with her. She had thought his silence meant she could push him around, but he needed to show her different. He reached for the cold handle of the door and jerked it open.

"If you don't come tomorrow, I will be very disappointed," the Book Lady said. "And *Lisana* will be disappointed too."

Trino just turned around and shot a mouthful of spit out of his mouth. It landed in a muddy splat on the crooked porch. Leaving the door open to the dusty heat, he ran behind the building and headed towards the highway.

The coolness of the bookstore washed away in big drops of sweat down his face and neck by the time he reached the access road. Taking noisy gulps of air, he slowed down but kept moving, even though he really wanted to sit down in some shady place. The best place for shade was in the park near the school, but Trino couldn't go there today. Rosca could be there. Waiting.

The guy was older and meaner than any other eighth-grader. Trino had heard all the stories. Rosca's rep was well known in the *barrio*. And Trino knew he didn't want to be the next guy wearing black to his own funeral.

Chapter Three
Home Boy

By the time Trino rested his tired black eyes on his family's white trailer house, the sun had melted into an old bruise on the horizon. The trailer park was noisy with Tejano tunes crackling from somebody's radio, a lady yelling "Mari-lena" like a howling cat, and some kid crying between whacks of a belt. Cartoon music blasted through the torn screen of their trailer door as Trino opened it and walked inside.

Gus, Beto, and Felix sat on the torn red rug in front of the TV, sharing a head of cabbage between them. Gus had to hold the white cabbage with both little hands in order to snag off a bite before Beto took it in his dirty fingers to gnaw off his piece. Then Felix would take it from Beto before his little brother got a second bite, and shove his teeth into the layers of cabbage. They ate without taking their eyes away from the robot reptile zapping at bad dudes with cardboard faces. The colorless cartoons swayed sideways and fuzzed out like fleas in the dirt. The TV had been a twenty-dollar bargain at the thrift store.

"Hey, Terrino, 'bout time. Where th'hell you been?" Garces lay on the faded brown sofa, his fat stomach pushing out the bottom of the Dallas Cowboys T-shirt he wore. He stared with red, swollen eyes at the TV, as he took swigs off a can of beer.

"I got busy," Trino said, then slammed his hand against the side of the TV, hoping it would clear the picture for his brothers. It did, just in time for a hamburger commercial to come on, reminding all of them that the boys were eating a cabbage.

"You make any money today?" Garces asked, and burped loudly.

Even if Trino had gotten lucky, he wouldn't tell Garces. Garces was a bum who needed to get off his fat butt and earn some money too.

"How much did *you* make today?" Trino said, and made sure he blocked the fat man's view as he stepped behind his brothers.

"No one picked me up." Garces waved his hairy arm. "Move. I can't see the TV."

No man who needed some day labor would choose a fat drunk like Garces. Or a kid like Trino either. Trino shook his head as he headed towards the kitchen area against the far wall. The sink was filled with dirty dishes. So were both sides of the plastic kitchen counter. Everywhere tiny brown ants helped themselves to spots of milk, crusty streaks of egg, and some brown crud that looked really gross. The cabinets were practically empty. No dishes in them, nothing but a can of coffee, a bag of corn meal, and some cans with no labels. A black marker labeled them as ten-cent specials, but often when his mother had brought home these cans, no one liked to eat what was inside.

In the small refrigerator, Trino saw a small plastic bottle of yellowish water and a half-gallon jug with a thin puddle of milk in it. In the drawers he found wilted lettuce, two carrots, a potato, and a plastic bag with stiff corn tortillas. On a shelf, behind a bread bag with a few slices in it, he found a bowl of beans. They were dried hard like a bowl of rocks. No wonder his brothers had grabbed the cabbage.

Trino shut the door, biting on the inside of his mouth. He had never felt like he lived worse than the alley dogs until Garces moved in two months ago. Calling himself

Cousin, Garces gave his mother the line that the boys needed a man around and he needed a place for "just a week or
so" until this big insurance check came in. "Then, I'll share
it with my *primo's* family, and we'll all eat like rich people."

When no check had showed up, Garces said he'd start
doing day labor, but if he made any money, it went to buy
beer and maybe a stale chocolate bar that his little brothers
had to split three ways. Lately, Garces helped himself to all
the food while Trino, Felix, and Beto were in school and
Gus stayed at the neighbor's.

"Hey, don't be a hog," Felix yelled, just as he jerked the
cabbage away from Beto. He put the cabbage under his T-
shirt, and said over his shoulder, "Trino, a guy was looking
for you. He came here three times."

"Dirty punk wanted to check inside," Garces said,
growling from the sofa. He followed his statement with a
line of cursing, and bragged that he told the guy off by saying he used to be a wrestler.

Trino rubbed his hand down his face. *Rosca knows where
I live. I'll never get away.* Was it even safe to stay here
tonight?

"I got my hands full! Somebody open the door!" Trino's
mother called loudly before he saw her juggling her purse
and two shopping bags in her arms.

The boys all jumped up at once, leaving the cabbage in
the middle of the dirty rug. Felix pushed open the door,
almost knocking their mother down. She barely got one
foot inside when Beto and Gus started hanging on to her
and begging for something from the bag.

"Did you buy candy?" Gus asked, pulling at his mother's black purse.

"Did you buy sodas?" Beto's fingers punched into the
white bag, trying to feel out what was inside.

Felix flicked a middle finger down on Beto's black
head. "Let her get inside, stupid!"

"Stupid, why don't you take a bag and help her?" Trino said as he grabbed Gus's arm and Beto's shoulder, pulling his brothers away from his mother. He grabbed the bag that Beto had been after and shoved it into Felix's arms, then took the other one towards the table.

He pushed away two empty cereal boxes, an empty cracker box, and more dirty dishes to find a spot for the bags on the wooden table that was surrounded by four mismatched metal chairs.

"*Ay, Dios mio*, it's hot," his mother said to anybody listening. She put her purse on top of the refrigerator, and came to where the boys surrounded the table. "Garces, did the mail come? Did you get anything?"

She asked every day, and every day, Garces said, "My check'll come *mañana, prima*. Then, we'll eat like rich people." He was sitting upright now, and with a loud groan got up from the sofa and headed for the bathroom.

Trino knew Garces left so his mother wouldn't say anything to him for doing nothing around the house. Instead, she yelled at her sons for being lazy. Trino had heard it over and over many times the past two months.

"*Ay*, look at this place. None of you could run some soapy water on those dishes? None of you can throw a box away when it's empty? I work so hard, and none of you can help?" Her dark eyes stayed on Trino's face longer than the others.

She didn't even wait for an answer before she slapped away Gus's hands, pinched Beto in the arm, and popped Felix in the back. Trino quickly walked around the table before she got him too. He started grabbing empty boxes to throw away.

She started unbuttoning the blue starched shirt over the black pants she wore to clean up motel rooms as she headed towards the back room. "I got a job tonight serving a wedding reception. Should get me the extra money I need for new shoes for Gus. "

"Will you make us supper first?" Beto asked, his black eyes watery from his mother's painful pinch.

"Of course, stupid." Felix said. "Why do you think she bought this stuff?" He shoved his brothers back to the TV. "Watch cartoons so Trino can clean the place up."

"And you get your butt back here and start washing dishes," Trino said to Felix, as the boy started to sit down by his brothers. Felix gave Trino a dirty look and got back up. But instead of coming over to the kitchen area, he ran his skinny body out the door.

Normally, Trino would have run after Felix and slapped him 'til he cried like Beto, but if Rosca was still in the area, it was best for Trino to stay inside. Felix probably knew it too, and that's why the lazy kid ran outside.

"You stay home tonight and watch your brothers, hear me?"

Trino's mother came back into the front room, snapping a faded pink housedress over herself. She had tied her black hair into a frizzy ponytail, which only showed more of her tired, brown face. Lately, she looked older than *Tía* Sofia, her oldest sister, who was fifty.

"I got to be back at the hotel by nine. They said I could sleep in the storeroom tonight." She headed straight for the sink and turned on the faucet. She let the water run while she rummaged through the bag for a box of *fideo* and a can of milk. "I won't have to pay for a taxi that way. Trino, you make sure you stick around until I get home tomorrow."

Trino didn't mind sticking close to home tonight, only he had no idea if Rosca would come back. Then what? Send Garces after him? Rosca would slice Garces into *menudo* and then go after Trino.

As his mother washed the dishes and cooked food, Trino killed ants with his thumb and wiped down the counter. Felix came back inside, only to have his mother hand him the full trashcan and order him to the dumpster. Garces didn't come out of the bathroom until good smells of bacon, *fideo, gorditas,* and some beans led him right to the table. Even when Beto had needed to go, Garces had told him to go pee in a bush behind the trailer.

Garces was scratching himself and burping along. He sat down on a chair that looked ready to collapse under his wide load. He sniffed loudly, laying his hands on the table, waiting to be served. Trino knew their mother would not eat as much because of the extra big mouth at the head of the table. As she set a plate down in front of Garces's sweaty body, Trino wondered again why she didn't tell that man to leave.

Trino spooned up his food directly from the stove onto a plate, and went to sit at the other end of the table since Garces often helped himself to the plate nearest him.

"Felix, where you been so long with the trashcan?" his mother said, as the boy came back in. She was serving Gus his food on a tray in front of the TV.

Felix dropped the plastic can by the stove, and wiped his hands down his blue jeans. "I was talking to Nacho and Carla. Someone robbed Mr. Epifaño."

Trino had been spooning *fideo* into his mouth until his brother's announcement. Suddenly, he felt like someone had a rope around his throat and pulled it tight.

"They beat him up with a pipe. Said it was three guys," Felix said, as his mother handed him a plate of food. He headed towards the couch, no doubt to keep his food out of Garces's reach too.

"Is Mr. Epifaño alive?" Their mother made a sign of the cross over her chest and shoulders.

"They think so. Nacho said the police have been at Epifaño's place all day."

"Where will we go to play video games?" Beto asked. He was sitting by Trino, but the metal chair was so low, all anybody could see was Beto's black hair and his eyes. He was tearing up a *gordita* and eating it piece by piece.

Trino shrugged his shoulders, keeping his eyes down on the plate.

Epifaño's store was just a hole in the wall. A few groceries, beer and sodas, and four video machines in a little room behind the ice machine. Trino didn't like the games much, but it was easy to shake them off their legs and get a few free games.

Today, he had gotten a free game of Kyper Killers, and had been close to getting the highest score. But Zipper and Rogelio had wanted to leave. He had waved them off, concentrating only on the fighting figures on the screen.

No telling how long he played it until he realized the sounds of hitting and punching were coming from the front of the store, not the game. Trino ran from the room, stopping next to the freezer in time to see Rosca slamming a pipe down on old Epifaño's head. The gray-haired man was bleeding from his face and a gash across his chest.

Rosca and Trino met eye to eye for a second, before Trino split from the freezer, heading for the door. All he had heard behind him was crashing glass as the front store window shattered. The bloody pipe had landed only inches from Trino's running feet.

Trino had no idea what Rosca and his gang had been after at Mr. Epifaño's store, but now they were after Trino, and Trino had no where to hide. He had hidden in the book store today, but what would he do about tomorrow?

"Terrino, if you ain't gonna eat, give me your *plato*," Garces said loudly, his fat arm reaching across the table.

From out of nowhere, a greasy fork speared into the side of Garces's hand. His arm coiled back like a rattlesnake. The man shoved his thumb and finger into his mouth. He sucked on them, looking at his *prima* with widened red-rimmed eyes.

"Leave my boys to eat their *comida*. They need their food, Garces." Trino's mother pointed her fork at her husband's cousin. She had taken the chair next to him. "If you feel hungry, then you need to buy *carne*, not *cerveza*, when you get a few dollars."

Trino wanted to give his mother a high five, but instead began eating the supper she had worked to fix for her family. With the same kind of defiance his mother showed, Trino wanted to stand up to Rosca, tell him that Trino Olivares was no squealer. If Trino could just keep out of reach 'til the heat was off, maybe Rosca would see that for himself.

There were few places where Rosca wouldn't find him. He had lucked out today when he found the bookstore, and until he found a better option, it still might be the best place to hang out. What would he tell the Book Lady? Another book report? Even though his stomach was getting full, Trino's head felt like he was running on empty.

Chapter Four
Slice of Life

It should have been a night for Trino to sleep well. He got to lie in his mother's bed instead of sharing one with Beto. Even though Gus was there, the little boy hardly moved all night, unlike Beto, who squirmed and kicked in his sleep like a kid caught by a gang. And Garces had gone off with two men and hadn't returned. That meant Garces's snoring couldn't keep Trino awake either.

Yet every time someone walked by, crunching through the gravel in the trailer park, or a car light reflected in the small trailer windows, Trino's heart started pounding. He'd raise himself up on the bed, then open a crack between the crooked blinds to see if he recognized anybody coming towards the trailer. Three different times he got up and checked to be sure the door was locked tight. His eyes finally closed only to open suddenly and see daylight breaking through the windows.

Trino felt sore and tired as he walked barefoot into the living room. Everything seemed quiet, even safe. Since Garces wasn't hogging the sofa, Trino flopped down there and stretched out.

The next thing Trino knew, Beto and Gus had their hands inside a cereal box, munching out as they watched cartoons on television. Both kids wore only white underwear.

Trino sat up and looked around. "Where's Felix?"

"Still sleeping," Beto said, then shoved a small fistful

of cereal into his mouth. Half of it dropped down his belly onto the carpet. Whatever fell Beto or Gus picked up and put back into their mouths.

Felix stumbled into the room a little later, only to put his head into his arms and fall asleep sitting at the table. Once Trino sat down with some milk and cereal, he shoved a foot at Felix's legs.

"Wake up, man. Oscar will be here at ten."

Felix raised his head, and squinted at Trino. "Too bad you can't come. Oscar's wife cooks good. His TV works better too."

"If things are so good, why don't you just live there all the time?" Trino said, working his voice to sound bored. "If Mom didn't have to buy your clothes, we could buy a TV that works instead."

Felix gave Trino the finger, and followed it with a few ugly words.

Trino always smiled when his brother cussed him out. It meant that Trino had scored one good, and Felix couldn't come up with anything better to fight back.

"You going to see Oscar today?" Beto had come to the table, a handful of cereal in his hand.

"None of your business, kid," Felix said, then gave Beto's shoulder a shove away.

"But I want to go," Beto said, his large black eyes moving from Felix to Trino. He slowly released his fistful of cereal on the table. "Why can't Oscar take me too?"

"He's my father, not yours," Felix told him, his voice starting to change back into that bragging tone he used every time Oscar's visit came around. "Your father took off three years ago. He's off some place, probably with another family."

"Why didn't he like this family?" Beto asked Felix.

"Ask Trino your dumb questions. I got to change." He stood up from the table, and headed out of the living room.

"Go watch cartoons, Beto. I'm hungry." Trino put a spoonful of cereal into this mouth, then leaned his head into other hand, hoping to block out Beto's pathetic face with his arm.

Every time Oscar showed up, Beto and Gus got very mixed up. How many times had Trino heard his mom tell his little brothers that Trino's dad was dead. That their dad ran off with some other lady when Beto and Gus were still babies. But Felix's dad lived across town. Felix had to go visit his dad once a month and nobody else could go with him.

But today their mom wasn't home. And Beto was still at the table, dragging his cereal pieces across the table's edge into his mouth, one by one, like he was going to stand there until somebody told him the way it was. Again.

Trino didn't talk to his brother. Finally, Beto ran out of cereal. He just went back to the TV, sat down by Gus and started munching again.

By the time Trino heard a car horn with a familiar honk-beep-beep near the trailer, he had changed out of the clothes he had slept in. Trino put on some jeans that he saw in a pile and the new black T-shirt his mom had found two days ago. It had been left behind in one of the motel rooms. Felix went off in jeans that Oscar had bought him last month, probably hoping he'd buy him more.

"Why can't we go with Felix?" Beto asked, once again, as Felix rode away in Oscar's blue pick-up truck. Beto's face pressed against the screen door.

"Oscar's got his own little kids to worry about," Trino said, hoping that would be enough for Beto today.

"Can we go play video games at Epifaño's?" Beto asked, turning his head and looking up at Trino with sad eyes.

"You got money?" Trino said, biting off the words in a mad way.

"No."

Trino hardly heard the word, as the boy lowered his face, and slowly walked away. Gus was rolling a truck with only two wheels across the carpet in front of the television. Beto sat down on the sofa, saying nothing as tears came out and down his small, brown face.

I hate my life, Trino thought, and pushed open the screen door. He let it slam before he sat outside on the cement step. He looked around for anything weird or somebody new, but the other trailers were the same scuffy ones he had seen for three years. He saw some kids about Beto's age kicking a dirty ball around and leaned back. "Hey, Beto," he called. "Flaco and Pete are playing out here."

Trino felt the edge of the screeen door pop against his back. He turned to see his brothers, still only in white underwear, pushing the door to get outside. "Hey! Put some clothes on! You want the guys to think you're still babies?" His hand pushed the door closed, and not much later, Gus ran out in a big T-shirt that belonged to Garces. Beto came out wearing some shorts, but no shirt.

"Wait!" Trino grabbed both kids by the shoulders and dragged them back into the trailer house. If his mother came home, and saw the boys like that, she'd yell at Trino. So many times, she had said, "I work hard to buy you clothes. I better see you wear them."

Trino was still sitting on the step, watching the kids, when he heard a loud car horn. A long, white car waited for the kids to move so it could come into the trailer park. The car was old-fashioned and needed a paint job. It had probably belonged to a rich guy once, but now rumbled towards Trino's trailer like it was going to cough up something gross and then die.

Trino saw his mother and that tall guy named Nick inside the car. Nick worked the motel nightshift, and sometimes gave his mom a ride home when she slept over after an extra job. Usually, he just left her off with a wave and drove away. This time that old car stopped and shut down in front of Trino's trailer.

"Hey, Trino! Come give your mother a hand," Nick called, as he got out of the driver's door.

How had Nick remembered his name? Trino wondered. He stood up as his mom got out of the car door with a white box in her hands.

"We got lucky," she said, smiling. She put the box in Trino's hands. "The people didn't want the leftover sandwiches. We also got half of the groom's cake, and half a layer of the bride's cake. There's even two jugs of punch."

Trino always liked the cakes, but usually the sandwiches were soft and soggy. Nick handed another two boxes to his mom before he pulled out two jugs of orange punch. He put them both into one hand, and held open the door for both Trino and his mom to go inside.

Trino thought Nick acted like a bellboy: being nice, opening doors. Nick even waited when Beto and Gus came running, calling out to their mom and asking about the boxes.

"Did you get cake?" Beto asked, bouncing through the door and running right to Trino, who barely set the box upon the table before Beto tried to open it.

"Get lost, kid." Trino grabbed his little brother's hands and squeezed them enough to make Beto stop. "Mom's not going to let you eat cake right now."

"Just cut him a small piece," his mom said, then laughed.

Trino's forehead wrinkled. His mom smiled at Nick, who had set the jugs on the counter beside the sink. Nick laughed with Trino's mom like no one else was in the room.

"I want cake too," Gus said, and climbed onto one of the kitchen chairs as soon as his brother did.

As Trino cut the cake, he watched his mom and Nick, trying to figure out why the guy was still here. His mom went to change clothes, and Nick sat at the table and put Gus on his lap. As Beto and Gus ate chocolate cake with their fingers, Nick started telling a story about a cat he had found last night in the motel laundry room. Trino licked the chocolate from the knife, giving Nick the *ojo*, just so he knew he shouldn't mess around with his mom.

Finally his mom came out in a red-flowered shirt and black shorts. Her black hair was loose, hanging around her shoulders. Her eyes were shiny, like candy dipped in chocolate. Usually when she came in after working half the night, she dragged around in a robe all day.

"Where you going, Mom?" Trino asked straight out. He put the knife on the kitchen counter.

"I need to buy Beto some better shoes. Nick said he'd give me a ride to the mall," she answered, walking behind Nick's chair. She slid her hand across Nick's shoulder as she headed towards the sink.

Trino eyed Nick again. Standing, the man towered over Trino. Sitting down, Nick's body looked average. Nick's face wasn't scarred up. No tattoos on his arms, at least from the elbows down. Since Beto and Gus's father had left, no man had been around much, until Garces showed up. And Garces wasn't much of a man.

Trino jumped when his mother's pointy finger poked his ribs.

"Listen, I said that I'm taking Beto and Gus along. While we're gone, I want you to stay out of trouble, hear me? We passed Epifaño's on our way home today. He got beat up by some boys with knives and a pipe. You better stay away from there, hear me?" Her brown eyes nailed him good and hard.

Did she know something? Slowly, he swiped his fingers through his black hair, before he looked at her. "I don't know anything about Epifaño. I got things to do today, Mom. I'll be back later." He hadn't planned to leave his house so early, but he didn't want her staring at him anymore.

Trino barely heard his mother call, "Be back before dark," before the screen door slammed behind him.

Without thinking, his feet took him towards Rogelio's house, a few streets down. Most of the houses on Passmore Street were old ones, with wide cement porches and iron columns holding up the roof. Some people, like Rogelio's grandmother, kept their homes clean and the paint fresh. Others lived in homes with no grass, just junk in the yard. Some parked two trucks in the driveway and another in the front yard, or left old sinks and stoves on the sidewalk.

"*Ay m'ijo*, Rogelio just left. He went to the store for me. He had to walk to the big Foodmart store since Epifaño's wasn't open today," Rogelio's grandmother told Trino.

He tried Zipper's house too, but Zipper's mom said he had gone to help out at the Tire Shop today. Trino thought about hanging out there, maybe earning a little tip money by helping Zipper's uncle change flats, but Trino didn't really feel like sweating over dirty tires.

Trino wandered around, breaking a stick up into pieces he could chuck them at stray dogs or bounce them off the sidewalk, then kick them off the curb. His mind wandered too, thinking about old Mr. Epifaño bleeding on the floor of his store, thinking about the deadly fire in Rosca's ey when he had seen Trino. Then he ran from Rosca and that crazy Book Lady. He thought a little about Lisana her friends. What were they doing now?

Without realizing, he had walked almost to th ack

parking lot of the big grocery store. He thought he might catch up with Rogelio going or coming. Now he had a place to get to and somebody to find. Since there was more shade, he cut behind the store, jumping over the plastic milk crates, thumping the stacks of flattened cardboard boxes that had been bundled with heavy plastic tape. He caught the ugly smells of rotting fruit, broken eggs, and spoiled meats. The tall black dumpsters against the brick wall were overflowing with the old food and trash from the store.

Trino picked up the pace to get away from the dumpsters, and shot around the corner of the store without looking.

He ran smack into Rosca's shoulder. There was no time to stop, run, or hide.

Wearing a blue T-shirt and sweat-soaked rag over his forehead, Rosca latched onto Trino like a trap. Two hands squeezed tight into Trino's arms.

It took everything Trino had inside him to give Rosca a stare that didn't break, even when Rosca snarled his name and shook Trino's body with one hard jerk.

"Where you been, man? Been looking for you."

Trino said nothing, didn't move, didn't blink. He tried to think.

Two other boys stood behind Rosca, but Trino didn't know them. All three of them weren't much taller than Trino. He might be able to fight them off, if they didn't stab him first.

Rosca had a small, rat-like face, with tiny black eyes and a pointed nose. He put his face closer to Trino, and said again, "Where you been? Who you been talking to?"

"Nobody." Trino said the word very slowly.

"I don't believe you, man. Nobody saw us but you. If find you, they can come after me."

"'m not a squealer, Rosca," Trino said.

Rosca pushed Trino back against the wall so fast, Trino's head slammed back and forwards. "How much can you take before you start squealing, man?" Wiry fingers clamped tighter into Trino's arms. A hard knee shoved all the air out of his stomach. Trino exploded into loud gasps and coughs.

Yesterday's fear suddenly hardened into a wall of anger. Trino fought back with every part of him, using his legs like a swinging bat, twisting his arms and shoulders free. Rosca couldn't hold him without help from the other two guys. The three of them pressed Trino back to the wall, but this time, he struggled harder to get loose.

"I'm not a squealer, " Trino said again, even louder. "I don't care what you did, Rosca. I got no reason to turn you in."

Rosca's little rat eyes started to get shiny. "So, you're saying I don't got to worry about you turning me in? Like I'm supposed to trust you? Just like that? Like you're my blood?" His dead rat breath filled Trino's nose just before Rosca's fist clubbed into the side of Trino's head.

"Hey! Take that some place else!" came a loud, angry voice.

Trino barely caught a glimpse of a brown uniform and something silver catching the sun, before he heard Rosca's words.

"This isn't over, man. I know where you sleep." Then Rosca shoved Trino to the ground. The three boys took off, running back behind the building.

Trino rubbed his head, heard footsteps. He looked over his shoulder, saw the uniformed man headed toward him. He pushed himself up to his feet, steadied hims against the wall for only a breath, before he took off r ning across the parking lot.

Chapter Five
The Book Basket

Trino didn't look back. What if Rosca and the others came around the store to cut him off? From the parking lot, Trino ran back towards his neighborhood, only to suddenly turn and run in another direction as Rosca's threat drummed inside his head, *This isn't over, man. I know where you sleep.* Trino couldn't go home right now. He'd be all alone.

So Trino ran several blocks, dodging old cars left to rust in the street, jumping over broken branches or trash bags blocking sidewalks. He ignored barking dogs and the old man sitting in his undershirt on the porch of a house, yelling out curses in Spanish. Trino's body felt ready to pop open and spill his guts everywhere by the time he decided no one was after him. He slowed his pace, then finally stopped running.

By then, the familiar part of his *barrio* was behind him, and all he could do was walk the same deserted places he had run past yesterday. Fear had controlled everything then. He had been so busy running and hiding that nothing else had mattered. Today he had time to think about how thirsty he felt, and how fast a bowl of cereal had disappeared inside his stomach, leaving only *hungry, hungry* in its place. And he had no money to get something to eat.

Trino kicked at the dirt road, only to have a sudden st of wind blow the dirt into his face. He paused to rub dust from his eyes with the bottom of his black T-shirt.

As he opened them, he saw a blurry set of shops in the distance. He almost smiled when he saw it: THE BOOK BASKET. The corner shop still looked junky, but Trino knew it was cool inside. It probably had a water fountain, or at least a bathroom sink.

Suddenly, yesterday's events came back more clearly. Trino remembered the Book Lady saying she'd have food for people who came to hear some man read poems. She had said he was coming at three o'clock. What time was it?

As he walked towards the area, he noticed there were about a dozen cars in the dirt lot in front of the shops. He looked around, trying to decide what to do. If all these people were in the bookstore, he might not get much food anyway. If the place was real empty, he couldn't just walk in and grab some food without the Book Lady saying something. He moved under a mesquite tree and watched the bookstore a while longer, wishing the place didn't have so much stuff in the front windows. Trino couldn't see anything.

He ignored the rumbling of bus brakes behind him. He stared harder through the window, still not certain if he should stay or just leave. A group of voices, all talking at the same time, made Trino turn around. The blue-and-white striped city bus had just let off two girls and three boys. They were heading in Trino's direction.

A hint of relief made Trino's body relax. He recognized the group of kids from yesterday. All he could remember of them was Lisana's name. He leaned against the mesquite tree, grabbing a couple of dry beans off the low branches to crack with his fingers.

The two girls offered him a smile, but he only gave a little one to Lisana in return.

"Hi. You came back." Lisana's brown eyes were shiny as she spoke to him. "Trino? Right?"

"Yeah," he answered. He didn't know what else to say.

He just looked at her, quickly noticing the plain pink T-shirt and blue jeans she wore.

The other kids were dressed like him, in T-shirts and jeans. Nobody would know he wasn't with them, that he didn't come for any other reason than some free food.

"Well! Trino. I'm Janie." This announcement came from the other girl. Trino noticed the ugly green nailpolish right away, because the girl started flapping her hands as soon as she opened her mouth and never closed it. "That's Albert, and Hector, and this guy is Jimmy. He's Lisana's brother. Can't tell they're twins, can you? Nobody ever guesses. Did you come back to see the poetry man? I don't know much about poetry, but Maggie always puts some great cookies and sandwiches out when she has a writer come to the store. If she didn't have food, Albert and Hector wouldn't even show up." She pointed out the boys beside her.

"Shut up, Janie," Albert said, dragging the words out. He was a skinny kid with a circle of straight black hair hanging over a shaved area around the ears. "Let's go inside. It's hot out here."

"Come on, Trino. We'll show you the best place to sit," Janie said, giving Trino a smile with a lot of crooked teeth showing. "If you don't sit close, some fat lady steps in front of you, or a tall guy gets in your way and you can't see anything. That happened to us last time, right Lisana? You remember that guy with the little red hat that smelled like cigars? Bleh!"

Trino hated girls who talked a mile about nothing. He stared at Lisana, not moving one step until he knew what she was going to do.

Lisana shrugged at Trino, then grabbed Janie's arm and tugged the girl along. "Albert's right. Let's go inside."

Silently, Trino walked behind the guys. There wasn't much to say. They were nothing like him, even if they too had come for the free food.

When Trino stepped inside behind the others, he noticed the cool air first. Immediately, his sweaty back seemed to drop away from his shirt. Then he saw that the front room wasn't just a dim place with jalapeño-shaped lights. Curtains on a large side window had been drawn back and lightened the room considerably. He hadn't even realized there were any windows before, but as he followed Lisana and her friends, he saw the curtains open on several small back windows in each room they went through.

Today, there were other people around. A lady with two kids about Beto's age were pulling books down from the shelves and looking at them. Three college-age women with longish hair and round little glasses on their noses were laughing in the corner of another room. Two men who looked like teachers and several other women who looked like sour-faced principals were also looking around at books.

Trino was a little suprised when he got to the back room. The shopping cart of books was gone, and so were the orange crates. The racks had been pushed back against the shelves.

It looked more crowded, even though Trino knew some stuff had been taken out. However, there was a larger space in the center of the room now. A blue carpet with crooked red designs was spread on the floor, along with the red beanbags and two big black pillows. Behind the rug, there were six metal folding chairs.

Trino didn't see any food any place. *Dumb idea to be here at all.* He shifted his steps backwards, slowly moving out of the room, but then a pair of women came down the ramp, bumping him back towards the girls.

He barely missed stomping on Lisana's feet. Before he could even mumble "Sorry," two tall men in weird-looking shirts, with sleeves that didn't even match each other, came into the room. Those three college types came in after them. A short man and a woman with ribbons braided through her long black hair came into the room behind them.

"Are we the only kids here?" Trino said. He hadn't realized he had spoken the words out loud until he heard. Lisana laugh.

"Doesn't matter." She turned around to face him. "Have you ever been to a poetry reading?"

Trino shook his head. "Not me."

"A writer came to my old school once, but what she read made no sense to me," Lisana said. "Talking about soldiers and windmills in some place. I like books about things I know. That's why I like Maggie's store. She has good books about people like us."

People like us? Trino shoved his hands into his pockets. *Who'd want to read that?*

"So what kind of books do you like?" Lisana pushed some of her black hair from her face. She continued to look at Trino as she spoke. She talked so easy to him, but his words came out slow and stiff.

"I don't know. Same kind as you, I guess."

Lisana laughed again, before she said, "Do you really like to read, or are you just telling me that?"

"I read," Trino answered quickly. He just hoped she wasn't going to ask him to give her a book report or anything.

"Oh, yeah?" Lisana studied his face as if she was trying to see the truth.

Only it didn't matter because suddenly Janie said, "Wow! Look at Maggie."

He turned around to see the Book Lady coming into the room with another man. The Book Lady's red hair looked shiny, even though it spread out in all directions like fire burning up an empty lot. Her blue eyes were rimmed in black, and she had pink smears on her cheeks. She wore a many-colored scarf over a green dress. The belt around her waist looked like gold nickels strung on a chain.

"Emilce is here," the Book Lady said in a loud voice. "Why don't you all find a place to sit?"

The guy wore heeled black boots, baggy blue jeans, and a blue-and-white striped shirt. His hair was like black straw, with a thick braid hanging down his back. When he turned around to face everybody, Trino saw the man wore a turquoise stud in one ear. His face was dark brown, and his nose looked like he had lost a few fights in his life. Trino guessed the man was in his thirties.

"He's not a hunk, is he?" Trino heard Janie whisper to Lisana.

"What did you expect, some guy from a *telenovela?*" one of the boys said, just loud enough for Trino to hear.

Trino stiffened when Lisana's soft fingers circled his wrist. It was like when Beto would try to get Trino's hand before they crossed a street. Often Trino pulled away from his little brother's hand, but Lisana's touch didn't embarrass him. It had only taken him by surprise.

"Come on," she said. "Let's get closer to the front."

Trino really wanted to stay right where he was, near the way to go out, but everybody started crowding around. Better to find some place away from all the weird people in the room and sit with Lisana instead.

Janie and the other boys had moved to a corner of the blue carpet near the flowered table.

Trino had always hated being near the front—it meant that teachers called on you first. Would it be like that in this place too?

Once Lisana sat down, Trino moved as far behind her as he could until the bookshelves poked his back. He relaxed a little when some old lady pulled one of the metal chairs up on the carpet near them. He could just hide behind her chair, and hope nobody would notice if he fell asleep.

He expected to be bored when the Book Lady started talking, but Trino felt curious about the man. The Book Lady had said that Emilce Montoya's parents were migrant workers. Montoya had spent a little time in prison, and now he was a college teacher.

Montoya's black gaze moved over the people in the room, as if he was trying to figure out what they were thinking. Immediately, Trino lowered his head. Rosca's rat face, Mr. Epifaño's bleeding face, Beto's sad face, and Emilce Montoya's gaze all mixed together in Trino's thoughts.

Suddenly, a dark, deep voice, captured Trino's attention. He raised his head, and watched Montoya begin reading from a slim white book. His poem was a blend of Spanish and English, words of the *barrio* people.

> *Why must our words blow across streets*
> *covered with blood of our hermanos?*
> *Scratched into prison walls, spray painted*
> *on fences, our words are hollow markings*

Montoya's chin came up, giving a full view of his bumpy face. He stopped reading out of the book, but he kept on saying the poem, as if the words were conversation between him and everyone in the room. He spoke about his neighbors in the *barrio*, described their suffering in such a way that Trino saw his own life. As Montoya chanted—*la palabra, la palabra, the word, the word*—until his voice was merely a whisper, Trino's mind echoed the words.

Then there was clapping, and suddenly Trino shook his head to clear the sound of Montoya's voice out of it. He looked at Lisana, who nodded her head as she clapped too.

Montoya read another poem that Trino didn't like much. It was filled with names of people he didn't know. Then another poem followed, one about riding from farm to farm to pick potatoes and onions, that made Trino feel angry.

Then Trino discovered Montoya's sense of humor as he read a poem called "Huevos Dias" about the mornings he and his brother went out to steal eggs from the hens without getting pecked or caught by a farmer's shotgun. And he read a poem about the wisdom of his grandparents that he called "Abuelos." Another poem that he called "Raspa Reruns" described his memories of eating cold, red snowcones; only the memory had come when Montoya was lying in a prison bunk sweating out the hot summer.

Trino looked over the room as everyone clapped again. The Book Lady was all smiles; probably glad there were customers to buy her books today. Lisana said something to Janie, then looked over her shoulder at Trino.

"Isn't his poetry amazing?" Lisana said, leaning backwards so he could hear her.

If she thought he liked it, she might expect him to read a poetry book. So Trino just said, "It's different from stuff in school."

"Isn't that the best part?" Lisana said before she turned away.

Montoya did his next poem in Spanish. His words were musical, like gentle tunes on a guitar, as he paid tribute to his brother, who had died in a war, but whose body was never found.

How does somebody stand up in front of strangers and spill his guts so easy? Montoya wasn't so smart, even if he was a college teacher. *Never let them know where to stick the knife.* Trino had learned that lesson a long time ago.

The poems stopped for a while, as people in the room started asking Montoya questions. One weird guy who didn't even know how to buy a shirt with matching sleeves asked something about finding "inspiration." Montoya merely shrugged his shoulders and said, "I find my inspiration everywhere. I can't tell you where to find yours."

"Do you think anyone can write poetry?" Lisana had asked the question, and didn't seem to care when all the adults stared at her.

Montoya's dark eyes set upon Lisana a moment before he said, "Poetry is about feelings. If you know how to feel, then you can write poetry."

Dumb answer, Trino thought. *Lots of things I feel bad about, but I'd never write a poem.*

But Lisana smiled, as if she liked his answer.

Montoya lifted his little white book then, and said, "I'd like to read a poem for the young people. Your lives make for the best poetry, because that's where the raw stuff is, the real emotions that make life worth the fight."

"Yeah, right," Trino mumbled, bending his knees to his chest to rest his arm across them.

"This poem is called 'Devil's Own,'" Montoya said. "I wrote it when I was eighteen."

> *Little brother,*
> *I gotta keep running*
> *from people who don't*
> *care if I live or die*
> *I gotta keep running*
> *spitting dirt, sweating*
> *from the inside out.*
>
> *I never asked for this*
> *sorry kind of life.*
> *I never wanted the devil*
> *chewing on my heels.*
> *He's biting through*

> *bones and blood.*
> *I gotta keep running.*

As Montoya read the rest of the poem, Trino was surprised to hear his life echoed in the words. *I wonder if Montoya's devil has a rat face, too* he thought.

Chapter Six
Montoya

After the poem about the devil, Montoya read two poems that were like nothing Trino had ever read in school. Montoya read a weird rhyme about sex and the desert sun. Another poem about a woman in Brazil with no eyes. Two poems about prison life made Trino think that a prison was one place he never wanted to live. The last poem was a funny one about the creation of underwear and the creation of poetry.

Once everyone had clapped, the Book Lady said, "Thank you all for coming. Emilce will be staying with us until five o'clock to answer more questions and sign books. I have refreshments in the side room. Please enjoy yourselves."

Trino jumped up as soon as he saw Jimmy, Albert, and Hector stand up. Since they had been here before, he figured they knew where the food was. And Trino was hungry, although not quite as hungry as before.

Jimmy caught Trino's eye and jerked his head towards the way out of the room. Since Lisana and Janie were headed up to talk to Montoya, Trino just went on his own.

"Weird stuff, huh? If the guys on the team knew where I was now, they'd get me good with the wet towels after practice," Jimmy said as they walked up the ramp behind other hungry people.

"So why did you come?" Trino asked Jimmy.

"Lisana likes this stuff, and our sister Abby won't let

her come alone. Hector and Albert think that hanging out in a bookstore makes them look smart." Jimmy laughed at his own joke.

If Trino had a sister, would he go to dumb places for her sake? He didn't know. His little brothers were pests, and every time he took them some place, one or the other would ask him to buy something he couldn't pay for. He usually managed to finger a candy and get it into his jeans before anyone saw him, but Beto or Gus usually wanted a toy, and that wasn't something that could be hidden in a pocket.

The four boys went inside a side room, a walled-in patio. Striped serapes, a poster of a *jarro* with large flowers, and several small clay figures decorated the walls. Two tables were set up, one with trays of Mexican cookies and little sandwiches like Trino's mother often brought home from the motel. Disappointing, since he was probably going to have soggy sandwiches for supper tonight. The other table had a glass bowl with orange punch and a large basket filled with taco chips. Nearby, two smaller green bowls were filled with a red, chunky salsa.

"How can you get anything on these plates?" Albert grumbled as the boys followed other people to the tables and picked up small round paper plates, no bigger than six inches across.

After Trino saw the guys each get two plates, he did too. Each of them filled up one plate with sandwiches and cookies, and the other plate with chips and salsa. Only problem was that there were no tables, and standing in a corner with a plate in each hand, it was hard to eat. So Trino put the chip plate on top of the sandwich plate and just pulled something out until both plates were empty.

That mouthy Janie had been right about the Book Lady's food. The sandwiches were firm and tasted like some meat was between the bread. The cookies were very sugary. Trino thought he should get a couple into his pocket for Gus and Beto before he left.

While Trino ate, he listened to the guys talk about a show they saw last night on television, and then Jimmy told a funny story about Mr. Cervantes, who taught math to most of the seventh graders. When Hector asked Trino his opinion of Coach Treviño's red cap with an armadillo tail coming out the front, Trino realized for the first time that Hector was in the same history class third period.

He had never been around a group of boys that had stuff to talk about. His friend Zipper never said much and Rogelio usually repeated what somebody else said first. Trino didn't say much, but inside his head, lots of words rumbled like distant thunder.

It was time for a second walk around the food table by the time Lisana and Janie showed up. Lisana held one of Montoya's white books in her hands. Her eyes looked like glass, and she was smiling like she had found money on the sidewalk.

"Wait 'til you see what Emilce wrote in my book." Lisana spoke in a whispery rush, before she opened the book and read, *"To a young poet, Lisana, whose words will take her as far as her dreams can soar."* She looked right into Trino's eyes, as if she expected him to be excited too. "And then he signed his name. Isn't that cool?"

"That's cool," Trino said, thinking he sounded just like Rogelio.

"I told him to come and meet my other friends," Lisana said, still smiling at Trino. "You should talk to him too. He's very nice."

What do you say to a poet? Trino just looked down at his empty plate. It was a good time to leave. He had eaten enough and he wasn't too far from the front door. He wanted to tell Lisana that he hoped he'd see her around in school, but didn't want to sound stupid in front of everybody. Maybe he'd give Hector a nod during class next week, and find out where they all hung out during lunch.

"I have to go," Trino said to Lisana. "I've got things to do."

"You do?" Her eyes got darker as she sighed. "That's too bad. But I'm really glad you came today."

She talked like she meant every word. Trino had never met a girl like that. Usually they called him names or made like he wasn't there. They talked like Janie or they laughed like donkeys. How did Lisana come to be so different?

Trino stepped back from her, bumping into a tall plastic trash can. He tossed his plate inside, wishing he could get a glass of punch now, but knowing he had to leave while he could. As he moved to go, he was surprised when Jimmy told him, "See you around." Albert said, "Be looking for you in school now, man." And Hector told him, "See you in history class, Trino." Janie just giggled, but Lisana said, "I hope I'll see you Monday at school, Trino."

Lisana's pretty smile gave Trino a good feeling he hadn't felt in a long time. Only he wasn't expecting the busy group of people filling up the narrow aisle that led past the counter and towards the door. About six people were lined up to pay for books, and the Book Lady was taking her time talking to every one of them. What if she saw him leave without buying anything? She couldn't be so crazy to expect everybody to buy a book today, but Trino really didn't want to have to talk to her.

Trino decided to look for a back door. There had to be some way to take trash outside. He slipped past the side room. Lisana and her friends didn't see him pass by. He headed back into the room where all the picture books were. He stopped and studied the room a little more carefully, but it was mainly shelves on the walls.

Without thinking, he headed down the ramp, only to

come back into the room stuffed with books and right into the last woman talking to the poet. Both were heading out of the room, probably towards the food.

Trino stepped sideways, wishing he could just melt into the bookshelves and seep through the walls. *Why did I even come here?*

Montoya paused beside Trino's stiff body and said to the woman, "I'll meet you up front in a minute. I forgot something on the table."

The lady smiled at Montoya, even smiled at Trino, and went up the ramp, holding one of Montoya's books against her chest like it was protection or something.

So weird. It's just a dumb book.

"You come back here to talk to me?" Montoya's voice sounded curious. He lifted one black eyebrow as he stared at Trino.

"No." Trino stared Montoya down just like he had Rosca. "I was looking for the back door."

"Why? Did you steal something?" Montoya asked.

"No!" Trino's face suddenly felt hot red. "I didn't steal anything. There's only books in this place. Why would I want them?"

"Why does anybody need books?"

"You said it, man. Nobody needs books. I don't."

Montoya slowly turned and walked back towards the flowered table in the corner. "I used to think books were dumb too. That was before I figured out how to read them." He picked up a copy of his book from the table, then turned back to look at Trino. "Can you read?"

What a dumb question. "Of course I can read."

"No, man. Do you know how to read? Not just figure out letters and sounds, but get into the words and figure out what they're saying to you. Can you read like that?"

Trino stretched his fists through the bottom of his black shirt. "What does it matter?"

"It matters when a guy asks you to sign a paper and suddenly he's hauling you off to jail. It matters when a lady asks you to sign something, and next thing you know, your kid's going to be raised as some other man's son. If you can't read, man, people'll tell you what you ought to think, and that you can't do more than scrub toilets the rest of your life. That's why it matters, man." Montoya rolled the white book between his hands.

Trino saw the trail of scars, the roughened, brown skin, and long fingers. Had those hands once held a knife or a gun? Had they once squeezed tight around a man's throat?

"I'll tell you something no one ever said to me, son. If you can be smart about reading, nobody'll ever take what's yours out of your hands. 'Cause you'll know more than they do. You'll know how to protect what you love most."

Montoya's words made Trino feel like he was trying to look through a dirty window, but couldn't see anything. He squinted at Montoya as if it might help him see better.

"Here. Read this. Start here with my words." Montoya extended one of his thin hands with the book in it. "Try and figure out what's in *this* book."

Trino stepped back. "I don't got any money. You better find another guy to buy your book."

"You don't understand, man. I'm giving you *my* copy." His arm stretched further. "It's a little worn out, and there's some other writing in it, but you can have it."

"I don't want your book."

"Why? You think poetry is for queers?" For the first time, Montoya's face looked angry. "Or maybe some teacher tells you what you're supposed to think the message is, so you can answer some dumb test and she can keep her job? That's not poetry." He tapped the edge of the book against his chest. "Poetry comes from inside us. It's written to talk about our lives and our feelings. It's one thing *hermanos* can connect with, whether they're in a schoolhouse or in a jailhouse. I've seen it." He extended his arm to Trino again, the book in his hand. "It's a free-bie—from one brown-skinned man to another."

For the first time, Trino could read the black words on the white cover: *Flip the Switch.*

"Trino? I thought you had left already."

The pretty voice behind him was familiar, but Trino wasn't happy to hear it. Slowly, he turned and saw a curious look on Lisana's face. She still held Montoya's book clutched against her. And there stood Montoya holding the same book out to Trino.

"Wait." Montoya's strong command made Trino look back.

Montoya slipped a pen out of his pocket. He opened the cover of the book. He crossed out something written across the top, then looked up. "Trino, eh?" Then he was scribbling something down on the inside page, but Trino couldn't make out the words.

All the writing took just long enough for Trino's food to go flipping around in his stomach. Finally, Montoya finished writing and closed the book. He stepped closer and pressed it into Trino's hand. "This is your book now. If you toss it in the garbage, or read it just because you got it free, it's your choice, Trino."

Trino's hand squeezed around the book. *What happens if I read this? And if I don't?* He looked back at Lisana, who chewed on her lip watching both of them.

Montoya shrugged his shoulders together, then silently walked up the ramp.

"Weird guy," Trino finally said, once the man was out of range.

Lisana frowned at Trino. "He gave you his copy of the book, and all you can say is that he's a weird guy? When was the last time you got something really good for free?"

He could tell by her voice that she was mad, but he felt too mixed up to care.

"I got to go," he said, then followed Montoya's path up the ramp. He held the book tight in his hand. And if that crazy Book Lady asked him where he got it, accused him of stealing it, he'd just tell her where she could stick the book. Montoya could stick it too.

This time, Trino just pushed his way through the people in the front room, heading out the door and away from a place where too many people had messed up his head. *Books are useless for someone like me.* And the one in his sweaty hand was no different.

He saw the Book Lady look up when he passed, but he just kept walking until the door handle was solid in his hand, and he turned it and found the hot air of escape rushing to his face.

He didn't stop walking until he got to the mesquite tree, and finally, he had to stop and read what Montoya had written inside the cover of the book.

First, he had drawn a pen line through the hand printing of his name. Underneath he had scribbled:

> *Trino,*
> *Don't let the Man flip the switch*
> *and fry you. Read the book!*
> *Emilce Montoya.*

Trino looked up to see the dented garbage can near the parking lot. He wanted to toss the book inside it, and just forget it, but he couldn't. And he didn't know why.

Chapter Seven
Garces

Trino took the long way to get home. His mind was mostly on Lisana, a little on her friends. Sometimes Montoya's poetry words, or memories of Rosca's threat.

Trino used to think he had the most boring life in the world. The last two days had been just *crazy*, man, just crazy. Man, all the stuff going on, stuff he got sucked into by accident. He'd just have to be careful. It was like walking through a field of cactus.

Tomorrow was school. Could mean maybe he'd see Lisana. He'd see Zipper and Rogelio too. What would he say? Couldn't tell them about Rosca and Epifaño, couldn't tell them about the bookstore, or listening to Montoya. It'd be the same old stuff with the guys. Laughing at the weirdo kids, trying to pop the snack machine when the teachers weren't looking, or just sitting some place and chewing on the grass.

Trino wasn't sure about his old boring life. He hated the problems with Rosca, but talking with the other boys today, listening to some of the stories that Montoya had told in his poems, and getting to know a girl like Lisana had put something new into his life. He wasn't ready to let it go.

He reached into the back pocket of his blue jeans and pulled Montoya's book out. He read again the words that Montoya had written just for Trino's sake. *Don't let the Man flip the switch and fry you.*

Without realizing it, Trino's head nodded in agreement.

Trino heard his mother's yelling coming through the torn screen door long before he climbed the step up. She sounded really mad. At least she couldn't blame Trino for whatever it was.

He opened the screen door, and quietly stepped inside, slipping behind his mother, who stood beside the kitchen table jabbing her arms around as she spoke in loud angry words. He noticed the white boxes she had brought back from the motel open and empty on the table. Trino's eyebrows raised up. Who had eaten up all that food?

Of course he knew, and looked up to see Garces sweating on the sofa. The man still had smears of chocolate icing on one of his unshaven cheeks. His dingy undershirt had the look of an old dishrag that he'd wiped his dirty fingers all over. He didn't seem to be talking much as Trino's mom yelled at him.

"I brought that food home for the kids, Garces. You ate it all. Didn't even leave a few sandwiches for their supper! How could you be such a pig?"

Garces just sighed, his reddened eyes looking like two shriveled tomatoes. "*Calmate, prima.* A man has to eat."

"What man?" She spit out her words like something hot burned her tongue. "All I see is a fat drunk who's been sleeping on my sofa, but doing nothing to help his family get a little food on the table. I want you out of here, Garces. Right now." She pointed her arm towards the door. "Get your clothes and get out of my house."

"You can't tell me to go, *prima*. We're family."

"Mom said you have to go, Garces. Now get out." Trino had watched in silence, but now that his mother had spoken the words Trino had waited two months to hear, he wanted to be certain Garces left before his mother changed her mind and decided to give him another chance.

"Stay out of this, boy. It ain't your business." His brown face flamed with a red tone that made him look slightly more dangerous. Only as he tried to stand, his fat legs were unsteady beneath him. He fell back into the sofa with a groan and a burp.

"Trino's here to help me throw you out. And if you won't leave, I'll call the police, Garces, and tell them that you stole money from me." Then she turned to her son. "Go get his clothes from the back room. I'll get a bag for them," she said.

Trino wasted no time in finding the few torn pants and shirts that Garces kept on the closet floor in the small bedroom Trino shared with his brothers. He was glad to get the sweaty smell of Garces out for good. As he returned to the living room with the clothes in his arms, Trino was ready to take on Garces himself. Trino had the strength to tilt a soda machine on its side to make it pay off. He knew he could shove Garces out the door if he had to.

"I was going to share my check with you, *prima*. Now you'll get nothing. *Nada, nada.*"

Surprisingly, Garces was already on his feet and heading towards the door.

Trino's mother muttered Spanish curses as she took Garces's clothes and shoved them into a black trash bag. She twisted the bag closed, then pushed it into the man's hands.

"Don't come back here, Garces. I'll tell them a bunch of stuff so you'll go to jail. Hear me? Don't come back!"

"I won't come back. When my check comes, I'll live the high life, *prima*. You and your boys had a chance for it too. Too bad."

As the fat man shifted himself through the trailer door,

Trino felt like pushing his shoe against the man's behind to get him out faster. Instead Trino enjoyed the sound as the door slammed. He smiled as he watched Garces stumble over the gravel in the parking lot of the trailer park as he made his way out.

"*Ay yi yi,* now what'll I do for supper?" His mother expressed a loud sigh, and Trino turned to see her sink into one of the kitchen chairs. Leaning her elbow onto the table top, she rubbed her forehead with her hand.

Suddenly, Trino realized how quiet the place was. "Where are Beto and Gus?" he asked his mother, and without thinking about it, started to pick up the empty white boxes on the table.

"Nick took them to the ice house for a soda. He said he'd get them out of my hair so I could do a few things around here. Garces ruined everything. I was going to ask Nick to eat with us."

Trino crunched a box in his hands. Who was this Nick guy anyway? Another Garces, to sponge free food off of them? "We have nothing for us. Tell the guy to eat some place else." He grabbed the other boxes, twisted them up and shoved everything deep into the plastic trash can by the stove.

When he turned around, Trino saw something that made his skin turn cold.

His mother's fingers were rubbing through tears coming down her face.

Trino had never seen his mother cry.

She yelled, she cursed, she hit, she gave the meanest *ojo* in the *barrio,* but through every bad thing that had ever happened, she had never cried. Why now?

Trino stood there feeling like an idiot because he didn't know what to say or do for his mother. Her thin shoulders shook. She seemed to stare at some invisible spot on the table as the tears continued. He wondered what she was thinking, her face looked so sad. He had always known what to do when she yelled or tried to slap him. *Run out the door as fast as you can.*

Rather than trying to run away, Trino felt a desire to step closer to his mother. If only he knew what to say, or what to do. Maybe get her a glass of water, if only to make his feet move and give his hands something to do.

As he set the glass of water upon the table, his mother set her damp hand upon Trino's wrist. Trino almost jumped.

"Thank you, *m'ijo*." She now squeezed his wrist firmly.

"You okay, Mom?" Trino could barely hear his own scratchy voice.

"He's been such a good friend to me. Now he's leaving."

"Who's leaving?" Trino asked, fearing his mother was talking about Garces.

"Nick. He found a new job. He won't be working at the motel anymore." His mother released Trino's hand to pick up the glass of water. She took a little sip, then set the glass down. "I've never known a man like him. He's very kind. He always thinks of others before himself."

Trino frowned. *Why is everything so crazy and confusing today?* The old familiar urge to run away tempted him, but he couldn't. Instead, Trino sat down in the chair across from his mother.

She raised her eyes to meet her son's. Tears and black mascara smeared together under her eyes. "I'm glad Garces is gone. He should have left a long time ago," she said.

Trino felt relieved she had gone to a subject he could talk about. "Garces was a bum."

"He sure was. But he's family. I felt I should take him in." Her eyes started to dry as she talked to Trino. "He was your father's cousin. Your father once told me Garces had saved his life. I thought I should repay him."

Trino shrugged his shoulders together. Her story explained a lot, but Trino didn't care much for either man. He hadn't known his father, and Garces had no qualities to respect.

He stiffened when his mother slid a finger under his chin.

"You look like your father. You walk like him too." She smiled a bit, but her brown eyes were still sad. "But you are not what he was. He always picked a fight. When I married him, I thought he was brave. When he died so soon after, I decided he wasn't." She gave out a sigh and then stood up.

It was more than she had ever told Trino about his father, more than he really wanted to know. The man had disappointed Trino's mother, and it didn't take a real smart guy to see that things didn't get much better with the other men who came along and left her with Felix, Beto, and Gus.

The loud crunching of tires on gravel made Trino stop thinking about his mother's problems and get up from the table. He looked out the screen door.

Nick's old car was now parked by the trailer. He got out to let Beto and Gus free of their seat belts in the back seat.

"Mama, look what Nick bought us." Beto's black eyes shone with excitement as he ran through the door. "See my new cars? Look, look."

Gus followed him, holding a green truck in each hand. "See, Mama, see? Tuck! Tuck!"

Both little boys waved their new toys at their mother, then went to the carpet to roll them around, making noises like car engines and crashing noises as the vehicles flipped over.

Trino was torn between a happiness for his little brothers, and a sudden resentment at the tall, dark-skinned man coming into the trailer carrying a brown shopping bag in his arms. *You made my mother cry. Not even my father ever did that.*

"Nick, you shouldn't have bought the toys. It's too much. You gave us a ride and bought us pizza at the mall."

Despite what she said, Trino saw a shine in his mother's eyes. It was just like one that showed his brothers were excited about their new toys.

"And what's in that bag, Nick?" she asked.

"Well, that barbecue place across from the ice house smelled so good, I just had to buy some sausages and ribs. Got enough here to feed me and three hungry boys. What do you say, Maria?" Nick looked down with a smile as his long arms held out the bag to her.

Trino's head battled with his stomach. He didn't want Nick around to make his mom feel sad, but those sausages and ribs smelled better than anything Trino had eaten in weeks.

"It'll be nice to have supper with a friend," his mother told Nick.

The man seemed to like to talk a lot as they all ate the juicy meat, baked beans, bread, and cole slaw. Nick had lots of stories that made Gus and Beto laugh and his mother too.

Trino was just glad Nick had brought the barbecue.

Later, he had wanted to look out the window when his mother walked outside with Nick. She stayed out there with him a long time. Beto and Gus were already asleep. So was Felix, who had come back from his father with five dollars in his pocket but no money for their mother.

Trino would have slept on the sofa, but Garces's smell had remained behind. How long would the sofa stink?

Sleeping with Beto was a wrestling match, but the boy smelled better. Through the open window of the small bedroom, Trino heard his mother's soft voice and Nick's deep one. It was those long silences in between that made Trino feel uneasy and sad.

But I still wouldn't write a poem about it, he thought just before he fell asleep.

Chapter Eight
Friends

Trino slid down in the scratchy auditorium chair, leaned his elbow on the wood armrest, and propped his head against his hand. Twice a month Ms. Juarez, the middle-school principal, called an assembly during second period and talked forever about raising grades and improving attendance. At least he had gotten out of listening to Mr. Cervantes try to explain fractions to the dummies who still hadn't figured out that pieces of pie and numbers could represent the same thing.

"Hey, they caught Fabian and Bobby spitting off the stairs," someone whispered.

They've been doing that stuff for weeks. Tell me something I don't know.

Suddenly, all the students around Trino started clapping. He slowly raised his head to look up, then straightened himself in the chair when he saw the girl who was walking across the stage towards the principal.

Ms. Juarez shook hands with Lisana, then gave her a white envelope.

"What's going on?" Trino asked the boy beside him.

"That girl's the outstanding student this month. She wins a free pizza."

Pizza? If I was going to be a good student, I'd want a hundred dollars.

But he kept watching a smiling Lisana, who waved her envelope at everybody, then left the stage.

Lisana had seemed pretty mad when Trino had left her in the bookstore. If he found her at lunch today, how would she act? Maybe winning a pizza would put her in a good mood.

"I was hoping Ms. Juarez was going to keep talking through third period too," said a boy walking just a step behind Trino after the assembly ended.

Trino headed towards history class. He glanced over his shoulder to see Hector, Lisana's friend. "Yeah, me too."

"Do you think Coach will tell another story about Cabeza de Vaca? Man, if Cow Head was my family's name, I'd try to get adopted," Hector said.

Trino shrugged, but smiled at what Hector said. Hector was a little taller than Trino, big all over but not fat. Usually he sat in the front of the class, and answered Coach's questions when no one else raised his hand.

Only this time, Hector followed Trino towards the back of the classroom and sat down across from him in the last desk in the second row.

"You think Coach will give a pop quiz?" Hector asked.

Trino shrugged, slouching down in the seat and putting his head down in his arms.

An unexpected rap on the head made Trino look up. Zipper slid into the desk in front of him, and turned sideways to talk to Trino. Despite the hot days, Zipper still wore a black leather vest with a lot of silver zippered pockets over his black T-shirt.

"Hey, man. Why didn't you wait for us this morning?" Zipper said.

"I had to take my little brother to school," Trino said, not wanting to tell Zipper the truth. When he walked with Zipper and Rogelio to school, they always passed Epifaño's store. But Trino wanted to stay away from that place for a week or two. He'd just use his brother as an excuse until everyone calmed down, especially Rosca.

Still, Trino had to say, "I heard some stuff about the old man who owns the corner store."

Zipper just said, "Yeah, me too."

Trino looked at Zipper, waiting for something more, but Zipper just sat there, fooling with a pocket zipper. So Trino looked over at Hector.

Hector nodded his head as if Trino had talked to him first. "You're talking about Epifaño's, right? You ought to see the place. Big board across the front window. His son—you know, the guy with teeth like Bugs Bunny?—he said three kids beat up the old man. Now ol' Bugs is standing in the doorway giving everyone the *ojo*. As if! No one's so stupid to beat up the old guy then come back to his store to buy a soda."

"Yeah," Trino said, his voice very low.

"So who asked you, buzzhead?" Zipper said suddenly.

Trino glanced from Zipper to Hector, then said "Leave him alone."

"Huh?" Zipper frowned at Trino. "Him? What?"

Before Trino could say anything, Coach Treviño walked in and announced that he was giving a pop quiz on chapter four.

Hector leaned over towards Trino, then whispered. "He always puts down three false ones in the middle. All the rest are true."

Trino looked at Hector.

"It makes the quizzes easier to grade. Everybody knows Coach does it this way."

I didn't, Trino thought.

When history class was over, Trino wanted to ask Hector about Lisana and the others, but Zipper stayed around since they both had English next. They always met up with Rogelio, who had the same class with them.

Only when Hector stood up and turned towards Trino, Zipper said, "What you waiting for, buzzhead?"

Hector rolled his eyes to the ceiling and just walked away.

"Where'd he come from?" Zipper grumbled, and Trino didn't answer.

He walked in silence beside Zipper, out of the class-room and into the noisy hallway. Bodies of kids moved like ants trying to get to the sugar bowl. One girl waved a dollar at another and two boys tried to grab it while others stood around laughing. Boys tried to get to their lockers, only to get bumped around. Somebody didn't see an open locker door and everyone heard the crash of body to metal.

The teachers started to bark their usual, "Get to class. Get to class, now."

Rogelio stood by a water fountain near their English classroom. His half-closed eyes showed he was sleepy, yet his wrinkled clothes looked like'd he slept in them.

"What's up? You look like crap," Zipper said, nudging Rogelio's ribs with his elbow.

"Crap," Rogelio said, then looked at Trino. "What's up?"

Trino shook his head. And the three of them stood there without talking, just standing by the fountain, wait-ing until a teacher told them to get to class.

Trino shifted his books onto his hip, and stood where he was, watching the kids go into different rooms down the long hall. A restless feeling burned inside him, like he should be doing something, instead of just killing time by a water fountain. But what?

Then down the hallway he saw Lisana and that dumb Janie coming towards him. They walked with one other girl Trino didn't know.

Lisana wore a short blue dress and shiny black shoes, as if she knew she had to dress up to shake hands with the prinicipal. She hugged her books and black binder to her chest as she walked with the other girls, getting closer to the spot where Trino stood.

His heart fired up, like the neighbor's old Ford when he worked on the engine. Trino licked his lips as he stared at Lisana, wanting her to see him.

Although she was speaking to the girls, her eyes wandered down the hall and for a moment met with Trino's. As she listened to what one girl said, she looked more directly at him.

He kept up a steady look, hoping she wouldn't shoot him down. He almost smiled as Lisana gave him a nod and a half-smile, something more friendly than he expected.

"Hey, pizza girl! Can I have a bite?" Zipper's loud call made Lisana's mouth drop open into an upside down U.

"Can I have a bite?" Rogelio called, following Zipper's lead. "Pizza girl! Pizza girl!"

All three girls stopped a moment before Lisana's dark eyes hardened into angry bullets aimed for Trino and the boys beside him. The other two girls looked like they had swallowed *jalapeños*.

Zipper and Rogelio howled like a couple of coyotes. Zipper nudged Trino, as if he wanted to remind him to laugh too. Trino's hand clenched into a tight fist as he saw Lisana push the other girls towards the classroom three doors away. She stopped just inside the doorway and gave Trino one final look that had *drop dead* written all over it.

Trino turned on his heel, shoving Zipper into Rogelio. "What's wrong with you, guys?"

"What's wrong with you? She's just a school type. What gives, Trino?" Zipper's brown eyebrows lowered into his nose whenever he got mad. "She wouldn't even spit on your shoes."

Trino's whole body felt as tight as a rubber band pulled to a breaking point. He wanted to punch Zipper and knock the spit out of Rogelio. Only their past history together stopped him. They had hung around together since fourth grade, playing in the streets and looking for pennies in the gutter. They had taught one another survival tricks and always found a way to have a few laughs.

Trino didn't want to lose his cool. Then he'd have to tell the guys how he met Lisana, and that was all related to Rosca and Mr. Epifaño. *Couldn't talk about that. No way.*

He slowly unclenched his hand and simply said, "She seemed like a nice girl. Leave her alone."

"First, that buzzhead in history class, now this girl. What's this? Leave 'em alone? They're school types, man." Zipper sounded half-mad and half-confused. "What? You want to be a school type now?"

"School type?" Rogelio repeated.

Trino ignored both of them and headed straight into his English classroom. He took his usual seat by the windows, so glad that Mrs. Palacios' stupid seating chart put Zipper and Rogelio on the other side of the room. They couldn't give him any more grief sitting over there.

He pulled a pencil from his back pocket and pulled out the sheet of paper he had folded inside his English book, some old worksheet on verbs. He started drawing circles on the sheet.

Trino couldn't get his mind off Lisana. He couldn't get his mind on English when Mrs. Palacios asked everyone to copy the sentences on the board. He did what he was told but nothing on the paper ever made it through any brain cells.

By the end of English class, Rogelio and Zipper seemed to have forgotten about the "pizza girl." The three boys walked on to the cafeteria like usual, with Zipper checking his pockets for gum, and Rogelio pointing out the kids who wore stupid haircuts. Trino walked beside them, wishing he was any place else but school, especially when he walked into the cafeteria and saw Rosca with the two boys who had jumped him outside FoodMart. They sat with two other eighth-graders at a table not far from the snack machines.

"I'm not hungry," he suddenly said to Zipper. His hand reached for the handle of the metal door they had just come through. "I'm going outside a while."

"Not me. Lunch is the only meal I'll get today," Zipper said, tugging Rogelio along towards the line of students waiting to get served.

So Trino walked himself out of the cafeteria during lunch and wandered out by the girls' gym. There were cement tables outside. Sometimes school types read books there. The jock types shot hoops on the outside asphalt court.

He stood there by the chain link fence, watching the guys play awhile, before he leaned against it. He let his eyes drift over the dry patches of grass around the tables.

Then he saw her. Lisana sat alone at one of the tables. In one hand, she held a slim white book that Trino recognized immediately. He had one just like it hidden under a loose board in his bedroom. Lisana's other hand leaned against her pretty face, her arm propped up on the table as she stared in the distance.

Trino watched her a long time, wondering what to say. Would she even talk to him if he walked up to her? *Just say hello*, he told himself. He'd just be cool. Tell her hello and pretend it didn't matter if she said anything back.

His legs felt heavy as he took steps towards Lisana. As he grew closer, she lowered her head back to a reading position. He saw her lips shaping the words she read.

"Hello, Lisana," Trino said, trying to keep his voice level. He didn't even stop walking, as if he had some place to go and she was just someone he saw on the way.

"Trino—hello." Her voice sounded friendly. "Where

are you going?"

His steps slowed up. "Just checking stuff out."

"How come you're alone? Where are those two monkey boys I saw you with?"

Lisana sounded like a real girl. Trino's first impulse was to make a comment about her friends, but he didn't want to mess things up. She did say hello and stuff.

"Where are your friends?" he asked, then stopped on the other side of the table.

"They're in the Caf. Some days I just like to read out here." She dangled the book from her hand. "Have you read any of Montoya's poems yet?"

"Sure, I read some." He couldn't remember anything he had read, though. When he looked more directly at Lisana, he saw a smile on her face. "What!"

"You." She gave a laugh. "I don't think you read *any* of the poems."

"Well, I got important things happening in my life. I don't have time to sit outside and read poetry like you." He hated when people thought he was dumb.

"Look, come here." She scooted over on the cement bench. "I want to ask you about this poem."

Trino frowned at her, but since she had made room for him, he just walked around the table to sit beside her. His heartbeat seemed to be throbbing down his arms and legs as she moved closer and placed the book between them on the table.

The breeze carried the scent of her hair into his nose. Smelled like flowers, nice. Her face had no zits on it, her lips were a pale pink color. Her dark eyebrows raised up when she turned to look at Trino.

"So what do you think he meant?" she asked pointing to a line of words on the page.

"Wh—what?" All he knew was that some of her soft black hair had brushed his face as she flipped it back behind her shoulders.

"Trino, look. *Here.* Read this and tell me what you think it means," she said.

Trino looked at the words, his fingers scratching through his black hair. The words were easy enough to read. But he didn't know if they were supposed to mean anything.

"Look, I'll read it to you," Lisana said, sounding impatient. "Maggie says that poetry is best when it's read out loud."

> With your eyes upon me,
> I'm someone different.
> I feel like I did when
> I used to believe a wish
> on birthday candles always came true.
> If I get a chance, I'm going to be your friend.
> I don't want to eat my birthday cake alone.

Lisana looked up from the book, staring right into Trino's black eyes. "I'm not sure. Is this a love poem, or just something happening between friends? Does it mean he doesn't believe in wishes? Or this other friend helps him believe in wishes? I don't know. What do you think?"

Trino shrugged, feeling kind of silly talking about what she read. "I guess it's a poem about friends. He uses the word *friend.*"

She smiled, then, and suddenly Trino didn't feel silly anymore. *I think Montoya knows what it's like when someone like Lisana shows up.* And he found himself smiling back at her. It's seemed like the easiest thing in the world.

She asked him about some of the teachers, a song she heard on the radio, and talked about her brother Jimmy's basketball team. At first, he'd only answer her questions, but eventually he got curious enough to ask questions too. By the time the bell rang, ending the lunch period, Trino felt like he and Lisana could talk about anything and it would be okay with her.

Later that night, while his brothers snored away in the bedroom, Trino sat at the kitchen table looking again at the poem Lisana had read to him. He whispered the words to himself, thinking about the poem and thinking about Lisana at the same time.

> *If I get a chance, I'm going to be your friend.*
> *I don't want to eat my birthday cake alone.*

Chapter Nine
Slack Time

As much as Trino wanted to talk to Lisana again, nothing worked out right for the rest of the week. It rained steadily for three days, and everyone crowded into the cafeteria during lunch. It was hard enough to find a spot to eat, much less find someone special to talk to.

Zipper and Rogelio were always close by. What would they say if he told them he wanted to talk to a girl? What did it matter? She wasn't in the cafeteria anyway. Did she go to the library during lunch? What would the guys think if he went there instead of eating? *What, you turning into a bookworm? You stupid or something?*

And Trino had to look out for Rosca too, just waiting to finish up the job he had started outside FoodMart. Rosca and a trio of eighth-graders always managed to pass down the hall as Trino walked from one class to another. Trino avoided eye contact. He still heard a low hiss, like a snake's. No matter how noisy the hallways, that whispery sound slithered into Trino's ears, down his throat, and coiled into a thick knot in his stomach.

Trino stayed away from the places where eighth-graders hung out, like behind the boys' gym or in the grassy area between the wood shop and the fields. He quit drinking water during the day so he wouldn't need to go to the bathroom at school. He didn't stand with Zipper and Rogelio by the water fountain between classes since it only made him feel more thirsty.

By the end of the week, Zipper started giving Trino a hard time. "What? You can't hang out anymore?"

It was Friday afternoon. Trino walked a fast pace, anxious to get away from the school grounds. *Just in case.* Zipper and Rogelio were like flies buzzing around a watermelon.

"What you trying to do, man? Score some points from teachers 'cause you get to class early? You want to win the next Pizza Girl award or what?"

"Just don't feel like standing around," Trino said. "I got stuff to do."

"Stuff? We used to do stuff together, man," Zipper said. "Now you just go home. What's up? You hiding from somebody?"

"Hiding from somebody?" Rogelio repeated.

Yeah, a five-foot rat's on my tail. Trino stared at the ground, focusing on his worn dirty sneakers and the cracked sidewalk. "Just staying home, that's all."

"For what? Waiting for your mom to come home and say that she won the lottery?" Zipper said, then spit on the sidewalk.

"Yeah, I'm just waiting for that." Trino's throat felt so dry.

"Come on, let's go pound out a few free games at Epifaño's. I got a quarter to get us started," Zipper said, unzipping the pocket over his left hip.

"Somebody told me that Epifaño's son is in charge of the place now. He'll be on top of us every second," Trino said.

"So? So we won't finger a candy bar this time. We can still get a few games without him knowing," Zipper answered, and when Trino shook his head, Zipper got mad.

"What's wrong with you, Trino? You still mad 'cause Rogelio and I left you back at Epifaño's last week? What?

You wanted me to watch and see if you could beat the last guy and type your letters up on the game screen? That could have taken all night."

"The top initials on the screen were yours. You didn't want to see my name above it on the Kombatants list," Trino told him as anger from last weekend's argument started to spread like a fever across his face.

"You're full of it. I couldn't wait around all night for you," Zipper said, his voice sounding tight and mean.

"Whatever," Trino replied, shoving his fists into his jeans pockets. He didn't feel like starting a fight. He needed to keep his head sharp for Rosca, not waste his energy on Zipper and a stupid video game.

But Trino was still curious about Epifaño's. Yesterday the neighbor had told Trino's mom that Epifaño was still in bad shape at the hospital. Said he couldn't talk to the police yet, hadn't found the guys who beat him up. *You're safe in the hospital, old man. Stay there a while.*

The three boys walked on with no more talking, just kicking stuff off the sidewalk. Finally everybody said, "Later," as they got close to the trailer park, and Trino crossed the street and went home alone.

The weekend loomed before him like a big yawn. With no plans and no money, he'd get stuck hitting the side of the TV all weekend, trying to find a picture that wasn't too fuzzy to watch. As Trino walked through the gravel lot of the trailer park, he saw Beto and his friends kicking around a ball, and wished he could be a little kid again, playing all day.

When he went inside the family's trailer, Felix and his friend Nacho were sitting at the table fiddling with a radio the size of a toaster, trying to get it to work.

"Wish we had some tools," Felix said.

"Where'd you get that?" Trino asked, heading towards the sink to drink all the water he wanted now that he didn't have to worry that Rosca might jump him in the bathroom.

"Found the radio in the dumpster," Felix said. "If we can get it to work, maybe we can sell it."

"If it worked, buzzhead, it wouldn't have been in the dumpster," Trino said, turning his back on the boys to open a kitchen cabinet. He looked for the biggest glass he could find.

Felix got up and opened up the drawer where their mother kept the forks. "I think if we scratched off some of the rusty spots inside, it might work. It's still got a good plug on it. Last one we found somebody had jerked out the cord."

Trino remembered when he and Zipper used to rummage through the dumpsters looking for good stuff. Every so often, they found some change, or a baseball cap. And they found old stuff like radios and tried to fix them up. Sometimes he wished he could go to school and learn about how stuff worked. Then he could fix stuff up and make some real money.

The tap water tasted warm, but it was wet. He gulped down the whole glass, then filled another until his throat didn't feel like a hard, dried-out sponge. After a third glass, he finally wiped his mouth with the back of his hand. At least he could drink water and go to the bathroom as much as he wanted the next two days.

His mom came home from work that night grouchy and tired, mad about some new manager who made her clean up a room twice because a motel guest found dead roaches in the sink.

"Ought to be glad they were all dead and not crawling around in the bed with her," Trino's mom grumbled as she banged pots and pans around, putting supper together.

Mom yelled at Felix for leaving his broken radio on the table and at Beto for getting his new shoes so dirty. She got after Trino for just lying on the sofa watching TV when somebody needed to take the trash outside. At supper, she was mad 'cause Felix didn't like the *calabacita* she cooked, and she griped at Trino for using up all the butter on his *tortillas*. And poor Gus got a few whacks for spilling his glass of milk on the floor.

So when that guy Nick knocked on the door just after they had finished eating, Trino was actually glad to see him. Maybe she'd yell at Nick for a while and leave the rest of them alone.

His mom got up from the table and went to the door to let Nick inside. "I didn't know you were coming—I have a little supper left on the stove. Are you hungry?"

"Hello, Maria. Hi, boys. Mmmm, sure smells good." He walked in with a smile on his face, something that seemed out of place after all the yelling, hitting, and crying the past hour.

Nick came to the table, and lifted Gus into his arms. Gus was still sniffing and rubbing tears off his face. "What's wrong with you, *niño*?"

"Nick, will you eat?" his mother said, coming by Nick and rubbing her hand across Gus' back, suddenly acting sweet like some mom on TV.

"I might eat a little, Maria. Actually I was thinking of driving over to the fair grounds in Perales. My brother's *conjunto* is playing there tonight. Do you and the boys want to come along?"

"*Ay*, Nick. I don't got the money to take the boys to Perales. What's the matter with you?" She returned to her grouchy self again.

"My brother gave me tickets for the carnival," Nick said. "And I got a little extra in my pocket from cutting down a neighbor's tree. Let's go have a little fun."

"Can I have fun, Mama?" Gus asked her.

"Come on, Mom, let's go," Felix said, just as Beto said,

"Can we go with Nick?"

"You don't know these boys. They'll want to eat everything. I just don't got the money, Nick," his mother said as if her mind was set. She started to pile Felix's plate on top of Beto's and Gus's and carry them to the sink.

Trino watched Nick put Gus back down in the chair, and with only two steps, the tall man stood beside their mother. Her back was to her sons as she rinsed dishes in the sink. Nick whispered something, and her head shook "No" two times. Then he slipped his arm across her shoulders and put his face close to hers.

Trino strained to hear what Nick said, but all he finally heard was his mother laugh. Only when she turned from the sink, her face was still squashed together like a grouch.

"If we go with Nick, I better not hear you crying for stuff we don't have money for. Nick's only got a few tickets. He's being very nice to take us with him. You better do what he says," she told them, wagging her finger at all of them around the table.

Do what Nick says? Trino looked at the guy leaning against the kitchen sink acting like he was something special since he had a few free tickets.

"Why don't you go change, Maria?" Nick said, as he caught Trino's *ojo* and stared back without blinking. "The boys and I can clean up the table and do the dishes real quick. Right, boys?"

It wasn't that Trino didn't ever clean up and wash dishes. It was just that Nick made the plans and expected them to jump and go. *Who does this guy think he is anyway?*

Trino stood up from the table. "I'm going to stay home, Mom. I got stuff to do." Of course, it was all lies, but staying home seemed better than being around that guy, Nick.

"Stuff? Like what? What have you got to do tonight?" his mom asked, putting her hand on one hip, like the teacher asking why he was late for school.

"Zipper and me got plans, that's all," Trino answered, starting to feel an itch creeping across his back. "We're going to meet at Rogelio's and hang out."

"Hang out? That's all you do. You'll just get into some trouble like those boys at Epifaño's and then what? No, you're coming along. You can watch your brothers. What if Nick asks me to dance a *cumbia?*" Then Mrs. Grouchy turned back to Mr. Free Tickets and gave him a little smile. She snapped right back to say, "And find some clean T-shirts for your brothers to wear. I don't want Nick to feel embarrassed if we meet his brother tonight."

Trino felt like a guy in jail. Everybody was giving orders and Trino had no say.

During the forty-minute drive to Perales, a small town known for nothing but big mosquitos, Trino got stuck in the back seat of Nick's white car between Beto and Felix, who both kept squirming around. And Gus couldn't make up his mind whether to sit in front with Mom and Nick or in the back, so he'd climb over and slide down right on Trino's legs and feet. Then he'd step on Trino's stomach so he could climb back to the front again. Nick told stupid jokes the whole way to Perales and he wouldn't play anything but some old Mexican songs on the radio.

Finally, Nick drove the car into some fenced-off field, already filled with a hundred cars. An old man with a flashlight asked Nick for two dollars, then pointed towards another skinny guy with a flashlight lining up the cars.

The sounds of carnival rides intermingled with the sounds of cars trying to get into the lot. The night smelled of exhaust, popcorn, corndogs, and dirt as Trino and Beto followed Felix and Gus towards the red, green, and blue neon lights of the spinning rides. He glanced over his shoulder and noticed that Nick was holding his mother's hand. *Whatever.*

"It's the Zoomer, Trino," Beto said, pulling on his big brother's T-shirt.

"Yeah, it is." Trino's black eyes moved over the tall ride with interchanging circles that left the riders in small white cages spinning upside down, shaking sideways, and spiraling around the track. *But it always cost too many tickets, little brother.*

They had all barely walked through the make-shift gate when some man called at them to try a darts game. Another man pointed at Nick and swore he had the muscles to knock over wooden milk bottles and win a stuffed animal for his little boy. Square white carts, brightly painted with pictures of corndogs dripping with mustard, pink cotton candy swirled on cones, and other delicious-smelling foods seemed to be everywhere.

The place was crowded, so Trino kept a tight hand on the neck of Beto's blue T-shirt. Whenever Beto would start to wander off to look at some game, Trino would jerk him back into step beside him.

He wished he had some money of his own to really enjoy the carnival. Nick was stupid to bring Beto and Gus here 'cause they'd just want everything. Gus was already in Nick's arms, whining about a stuffed dog and Beto jumped around asking for a ticket as soon as he saw the rides.

Knots of teenagers were lined up outside the rides that made you dizzy or put you high in the air and dropped you fast. Little kids were pulling their parents towards those dumb rides that did nothing but go in a circle. Each ride seemed to have its own music blasting from speakers, mixing into an earful of noise inside a buzzing head.

Trino lost his hold on Beto when Nick agreed to let Beto and Gus use four of the tickets on some ghost train. It came in and out of a black trailer painted with white fangs and purple eyes. Since Felix still had the five bucks his dad gave him last Sunday, he wanted to check out the faster rides.

"You can go look around, but Trino—go with your brother. And don't go any place but the carnival rides. You hear me?" his mother said. She glanced at her two older sons and then back to the black trailer. Nick helped Gus and Beto into one of the train cars.

Trino didn't want to hang out with Felix, especially since Felix would hog his money and never share it. Only Trino didn't want to stay with his mom and Nick either. So he followed Felix, using a shoulder or an elbow to get through the jumbles of people standing around, watching others screaming their heads off on different rides.

Glad his brother wore a bright red T-shirt, Trino managed to see where Felix walked, even when a couple of girls or the screams off a ride made him pause a moment to look around.

When they got to the end of the row of rides, Felix turned and waited for Trino to catch up.

"I guess I'll ride the Zoomer. Not much else I want to try." Felix spoke loudly over the roar of the rides around them.

"You going to use up all your money on one ride?" Trino said, frowning at his brother.

"Shoot, it don't cost no five dollars to ride the Zoomer," Felix answered. "You and I can both go on it with five dollars."

Trino smiled. "Thanks, Bro. Didn't know you wanted to buy me a ticket."

Felix gave Trino a mean look. "No way. Just 'cause I got a dad to give me money—"

Suddenly, Felix was shoved right into Trino's chest with enough force to make both boys stumble backwards.

Despite a slide off the gravel, Trino found his footing

and kept his balance. He grabbed onto Felix, jerking him aside, not caring if his brother landed on his butt. Only the sight of Rosca, and another boy with a fat brown face, made Trino grip onto Felix and shove his brother behind him.

"Been looking for you, boy," Rosca said, growling his words as he lunged towards Trino and grabbed a fistful of Trino's black T-shirt in each hand. "Who knew I'd finally get you in Perales?"

Chapter Ten
Zoomer

It only took a couple of seconds before Trino reacted. He raised his fists to smack against Rosca's shoulders. "Let go of me, Rosca." If he was going down, he'd go down fighting, that's for sure.

"We got business to settle, Trino. Right here, right now." Rosca jerked his hands, pulling Trino's shirt tighter around his neck. "Don't need you fingering me to the cops."

"Go, Felix, go," he said, loud and angry. "Get out of here. Now!"

But that fat kid grabbed Felix and wrapped one of his arms around Felix's throat. His other arm pressed hard against Felix's stomach.

Felix made a noise like a dog choking on a bone.

Although Trino had been so frightened that day in Epifaño's and during that hard run afterwards, he wasn't scared for himself now, only for Felix. How would he get both of them loose? Did Rosca have other guys around just waiting for a signal to join in?

The next few seconds were a jumble of groans and cursing, tugging and sudden freedom. The fat kid was on his stomach, eating dirt. Felix was wide-eyed, speechless, but standing alone. Rosca had been pulled off Trino's shirt by large hands that separated them like a crowbar. Rosca stumbled backwards, then rushed forward, only to be shoved back again by a solid brown hand. Rosca's rat face looking surprised, even scared. A solid grip squeezed on Trino's shoulder.

"What's going on here? What are you trying to do to my boys?"

The voice was familiar, only throaty with anger.

Nick stood beside Trino, his breathing heavy as he spoke. "Trino, you know these boys?"

He had to look up to talk to Nick. In the uneven lighting of neon lights from the spinining rides, the man looked taller than ever. His dark face, pressed together as it was, made Nick look like a man you didn't mess with.

Trino didn't want to mess with Rosca either. So he played it dumb.

"I—I don't know these guys, Nick. They got me mixed up with somebody else, I think."

Nick grabbed onto Felix and pulled the boy closer. Then he spoke to Rosca "Don't be messing with my boys. Get out of here, and don't let me catch you around us any more. Go on! Beat it!"

The other boy slowly got up. Rosca made a grunting noise, before he raised his arm and shot Nick the finger. He turned his back on them and walked off behind some portable toilets. The fat-faced boy ran to catch up to him.

Trino pushed his hand through his black hair and sighed, a few nasty words sliding out under his breath. Would he spend the rest of life waiting for Rosca to show up and kill him?

"You boys okay? What happened?" Nick asked, rubbing a hand over Trino's shoulder.

"Nothing." Trino jerked away from him. He was grateful the guy showed up, but he hated that touchy stuff. "They just showed up. Don't worry about it."

"But, Trino. I heard him say your name," Felix said, looking from Nick to his brother.

Trino's eyes narrowed as he gave his brother a silent

shut up. "I said they just showed up. They're nobody. Let it drop. It's over." Only inside his head, Trino knew different.

Nick stepped around so they faced each other. "Are you in some kind of trouble, Trino?" His voice was quiet now. "I'm not so old that I don't remember how it goes with boys. Only you kids today get into some dangerous stuff that can get you hurt. I'd hate to see that happen to you."

"I can take care of myself. What are you doing here anyway? Where's Mom?" Trino said, asking questions to take the attention off himself.

Nick slowly rubbed his chin, before he answered. "She's with the *niños.* I came looking for you two. Thought you two might need some tickets." He paused. "Or maybe some money . . ."

"We don't need anything from you," Trino said. Nick just wanted to make points with their mother anyway.

"I'll take some tickets," Felix said. "I want to ride the Zoomer."

Traitor, Trino thought, and turned to walk away from them. Only Felix and Nick followed right behind him. But he ignored them, walking through the crowd as if he had a place to go. He felt as if everything around him was spoiled by Rosca's appearance. He couldn't even go out with his family without running into trouble. *Life stinks, it really does.*

A hand pressed on his shoulder then, and he stiffened. *This time he'd really tell Nick to take those stupid tickets and just shove them—*

"Hi, Trino. I never thought I'd see you here."

He had turned around to find Lisana. Just behind her stood her brother, Jimmy, and Hector, who had stayed away from Trino in history class ever since Zipper had chased him off.

"Uh—hey—Hi, hi." Trino's face felt hot all over. He stared at Lisana a second, then nodded towards the guys. "What's up?"

"Just standing here in line for the Zoomer," Jimmy said. "Have you ridden it yet?"

Trino glanced around, seeing the large steel ride to his left, and then noticing the line of teenagers and some older people curving around the ticket booth like a snake. He shook his head and said, "No. I've been on it before, but not here."

Lisana's brown eyebrows raised. "Is it really scary? I've never been on it. This is Jimmy and Hector's idea. Not mine."

Trino wanted to make her feel better. He even smiled as he said, "It's scary, but it's a lot of fun. You'll like it, Lisana."

"Will you ride it with me? Jimmy and Hector can ride by themselves." She gave her brother a frown. "I don't want them to make fun of me if I start screaming."

Jimmy and Hector started laughing. Lisana just stuck her tongue out at them. Then she turned her pretty brown eyes back to Trino with a silent plea.

"Uh—" Trino turned around, searching the crowd for Felix's red T-shirt or a tall man who always seemed to be smiling. He spotted them a few feet away, standing at the end of the line. He looked back at Lisana and said, "I'll be right back."

Walking towards Felix and Nick, Trino felt like a wad of paper had been shoved in his throat. He felt nervous and stupid, worried and mad all at the same time.

"You got any more tickets, Nick?" Trino asked as soon as he reached the man. He looked up and gave Nick a steady look, even though his legs felt like he had just gotten off the Zoomer.

"I see you found some friends," Nick said, crossing his

arms upon his chest. "Do you want tickets for them too?"

Nick's offer surprised Trino. He might have given it more thought, but he wanted to get back to Lisana. "They got their own tickets. I need some for me."

"What about me?" Felix said. "Don't hog all the tickets, Trino."

Trino just stared at Nick. "I just want enough to ride the Zoomer once."

Nick reached into one of his shirt pockets and pulled out some green tickets. He counted off five, then tore them from the others and handed them to Trino. "Here."

"Later," Trino said, and started to walk away.

"Hold on there, Trino," Nick called, and when Trino turned back he saw Nick had some dollars folded between his fingers. "Take this too. You might need it. Meet your Mom and me by the pavilion where the band plays in about an hour, okay? And stay out of trouble, hear me?"

Trino shrugged and told him, "See you later."

"You're welcome!" Nick called out after Trino walked off, but he didn't turn back.

The next hour was more fun than Trino could ever remember having. Lisana screamed for most of the Zoomer's up and downs, spins and shakes, but she also clung to Trino. Her closeness gave him a sense of strength and power he had never felt before. After the ride, everyone laughed and shared the moments each thought was the scariest. Then Lisana and Trino watched Jimmy and Hector shoot basketballs into straw baskets, and after four dollars worth of trying, Jimmy managed to win a six-inch stuffed dog, which he gave to Lisana.

"Thank you, Jimmy. I'll love it all my life," she said in a little kid voice.

Then Lisana, Jimmy, and Hector watched Trino try the dart game. He broke only two balloons and was awarded a plastic football. Lisana tried a wheel of fortune, but her number didn't come up. Then everyone wanted a *raspa*, a scoop of flavored ice served in a paper cup. They ate *raspas* while watching some muscular man try to win a three-foot dog for his skinny girlfriend. He had to swing a big hammer down on a platform to ring the bell at the top of a tall pole.

They were debating whether or not to all ride the Zoomer again, when a thin woman who looked a lot like Lisana came up. She had a baby in her arms and Lisana introduced her as Abby, her big sister.

"I had a lot of fun, Trino. Thanks for riding the Zoomer with me," Lisana said, before they all separated. "And thanks for buying me a snow cone."

Trino smiled as he said, "I had fun too, Lisana. Maybe I'll see you in school on Monday."

"You know where to find me, I bet." She laughed and waved, then turned towards her sister. "Jimmy won this stuffed dog. Do you think Nelda will like it?" Then she shook it over the baby's face and giggled when the baby reached for it.

Trino turned away, heading for the wooden pavilion at the end of the fair grounds. He tossed the plastic football between his hands. He decided to take the last two dollars of Nick's money and buy some cotton candy for Beto and Gus.

He found his brothers, his mom, and Nick sitting at picnic tables watching the *conjunto* band. Two men playing guitars, a man on drums, and a singer who played the accordian sang a lively *polka* as pairs of dancers bounced along to the music.

Felix was at the next table talking to three other boys. Gus sat in his mother's lap, hugging a little red bear. Beto sat by Nick, looking sad, like there was only one prize and he didn't get it.

Trino rubbed Beto's head and said, "Look what I won

for you, kid." And he felt pretty good inside when Beto's black eyes brightened as he took the ball into his hands.

"You need to tell your brother thank you for the football," Nick said to Beto, putting his arm across the boy's shoulders.

Beto looked at Nick first, then at Trino. "Thank you for the football."

Trino nodded, then put the cotton candy on the top of the picnic table. "This is for you and Gus to share. But say 'thank you' to Nick. He gave me the money." Then he looked at Nick and said, "Thanks for the tickets, man. And—and for your help with the other stuff."

"You're welcome," he said, then pushed himself up from the table. "Music's good. I feel like dancing a few *polkitas*. Come on, Maria. Let's go dance."

Trino took their place between Gus and Beto, and the three of them ate chunks of pink sugared swirls as they watched their mom dance with Nick.

Maybe there's more to Perales than big mosquitos after all.

Trino tried to keep the good feelings from Perales inside him through the weekend and into the school week, but it was hard. Saturday and Sunday had been hot and boring, and the week at school dragged along worse than usual. He tried to find Lisana and talk to her before English, but Mrs. Palacios was gone. The substitute was a short, wide woman who looked like a guard dog in high heels. She barked at everyone to get to class. Even the other teachers, who often stood by their doors to talk a little, obeyed her orders.

A couple of those days, Trino managed to lose Zipper and Rogelio at lunch in order to check if Lisana was outside. But the two times he saw Lisana, a pile of girls were at the same table giggling and combing their hair. He just headed back to the cafeteria each time.

Friday, he sat with his friends, half-listening to Zipper's stupid comments about Mrs. Palacios's sub, stirring his fork through the runny red jello on his tray. He felt restless, anxious to change things; but he didn't know how.

Suddenly, Trino felt a sharp pop in the back of his head. Caught off guard, he wasn't expecting Rosca to grab Zipper by the back of his jacket and jerk him off the chair. Rosca sat himself down, and from out of nowhere, three other eighth-graders showed up. One behind a wide-eyed Rogelio, and two on either side of Trino. Zipper just crawled on the floor, trying to get out of the way before he got stepped on.

Under the table, Trino closed his hand into a fist. Carefully, he turned to look at Rosca without any emotion.

"Looking for me?" Trino said in a smooth voice, even though his lunch was turning into something thick and sloshy in his stomach.

"Things are cool between us, man. You kept your mouth shut." Rosca's face didn't turn in Trino's direction; those dark little rat eyes continued moving around the cafeteria, as if he wanted to be sure there were no cats around. "You want to do some business later? Get yourself some cash?"

"You need some other guys, Rosca? Me and Rogelio here—we're cool." Zipper's head and shoulders had resurfaced at the end of the table. Slowly, he stood upright, but his eyes seemed anxious, like a dog begging for a scrap. "Tell 'em, Trino. Tell him we're cool."

"We're cool," Rogelio repeated.

Are you crazy, man? screamed a voice inside Trino's mind. But he only said, "My friends are cool."

Trino kept his face like a stone mask. *Never let 'em see where to stick the knife.* He glanced at Rogelio. The guy had the same look of fear and excitement when they had ridden the Zoomer last year.

The loud bell, ending first lunch period, seemed to blare inside Trino's chest. He realized he had just been holding his breath, as he tried to stay cool in front of Rosca and the others. Slowly, he let the air out through his teeth.

"Later!" Rosca rapped his knuckles on the table top once, then stood up. With just a nod, he had the other eighth-graders following him out of the cafeteria.

"Hey, Trino, what gives? Why'd Rosca come to *you*?" Zipper asked as the three of them walked over to the side window to dump off their trays.

Trino shrugged his shoulders together. "I don't know." His voice was low, heavy with saracasm. "Just lucky, I guess."

"What do you think we'll have to do for Rosca?" Zipper asked.

"Who knows," Trino replied.

"Who knows," Rogelio said.

Trino whacked his fist into Rogelio's shoulder. "Can't you find your own words, man? Do you have to just repeat what everybody says, like a tape recorder?"

"Let's call him Recorder!" Zipper started laughing, which only made Trino madder.

Everything with Rosca had started because Zipper and Rogelio ran off and left him alone in Epifaño's that day. Now Zipper and Rogelio were all ready to go along when Rosca wanted Trino to do a job for him. Was it better to be Rosca's friend than Rosca's enemy?

Not much of a choice, Trino thought. He could smell the trouble coming towards him.

Chapter Eleven
Crackdown

The next week Rosca made daily contact. When they passed in the halls, Trino looked at Rosca with a raised eyebrow and slight bow of his chin. In the cafeteria, Rosca would rap the table top or give Trino a knock in the shoulder with his knuckles. Trino merely slapped his hand twice on the table top as a response, just enough to acknowledge him; hoping it wouldn't be mistaken for anything more.

As for Rogelio and Zipper, every time Rosca appeared, it was like they swallowed some dope that made them into different people. Each day, Zipper's comments about other kids got meaner and louder. Of course, Rogelio repeated them, making things worse. Zipper flipped the finger more often and put more four-letter words into his talk. Rogelio did too.

On Thursday, Rogelio drew a naked woman on an old worksheet and labeled it *Mrs. Palacios*. He passed it around class until she got hold of it. Rogelio just gave a big smile when Mrs. Palacios' face turned a deep red color. He got sent to the front office and Trino didn't see him the rest of the day. That same afternoon, Zipper picked a fight with a seventh-grader during P.E. and Coach Menchaca sent him to cool off in the vice-principal's office.

After school, both boys jumped on Trino for not helping them out.

"If you had held Bobby against the wall like I wanted

you to, I could have popped him good before Menchaca showed up. Why did you just stand there?" Zipper said, his voice sharp with anger.

"Why didn't you tell Mrs. Palacios it wasn't my paper?" Rogelio told him, popping Trino in the arm like Rosca had done in the cafeteria that day.

Only Trino didn't take it from Rogelio. He shoved Rogelio so hard the boy fell off the curb and stumbled into the street.

"It *was* your stupid paper. Next time erase your name, before you start drawing naked teachers." Trino felt like his hair was on fire as he turned on Zipper. "And if you can't handle your own fights, then don't start 'em. You talk trash, then expect me to back you up. I got better things to do."

So Zipper flipped Trino the finger, and Rogelio actually said some four-letter words that Zipper hadn't said first. Trino spit out his own curses in English and Spanish before he crossed the street to get away from both of them.

Still they shouted more, even some junk about Trino's mother. So Trino turned into an alley and walked faster, anxious to get away. His ragged breathing hurt as it came out. Hadn't the three of them always said that Rosca was bad, bad trouble? What was wrong with Zipper and Rogelio? Did they want to be like Rosca now? Did Trino?

Thoughts of Mr. Epifaño's bleeding face suddenly appeared again. The old man's groans echoed inside Trino's head.

He slowed his walking, and wandered through familiar neighborhoods, trying to figure out something to do about his old friends and Rosca. Just questions. No answers.

Then suddenly, Trino stood only a few steps away from the corner store with the large board across the front. His first impulse was to run away. However, he stood where he was. He felt *maracas* shaking inside of him.

There on the sidewalk in front of Epifaño's store, Trino remembered when he ran out of the store trying to save his own skin. The old man hadn't ever hurt anybody in the neighborhood, even let some people charge a little if they were low on cash. Even Trino's mom had needed credit sometimes.

Not that Trino was going to be some hero and tell the police about Rosca. But Trino could at least ask about the old man, see how things turned out.

Slowly, Trino pushed the silver bar on the glass door to let himself into the store. It was hard to see anything at first. The place looked darker since the front window was boarded over. The store smelled sour and sweaty, like old pickles wrapped in one of Garces' T-shirts.

Shelves on the four aisles of food, soaps, and car stuff looked a little empty, as if the person who had taken over for the old man wasn't doing a very good job replacing what had been sold. Trino saw the tall man sitting on a stool behind the wooden counter reading a car magazine. As the man looked up at him, Trino suddenly remembered Hector's description and almost smiled. The old man's son *did* look like Bugs Bunny, with his buck teeth pushing out under a fuzzy brown mustache.

"What you need, boy?"

Trino thought of a lie quick enough. "My mom needs *comino*. Sometimes Mr. Epifaño has some."

"Over there. By the salt." The man resumed his looking at the pictures.

"Uh—my mom—she's wondering. Is Mr. Epifaño okay?"

The man looked up with an angry glare. "He's in the damn hospital, boy. Some punks like you beat the crap out of him for a few lousy dollars. This place is a rat hole." Then he spit some brown stuff on the floor, and covered up his flat, bumpy nose with the magazine.

Trino thought asking about the old man would make him feel less guilty, but it hadn't. The *maracas* he had felt earlier were now empty and still.

He wondered if it was planned that both Zipper and Rogelio were not in school on Friday. Rosca was there, however, with his hallway eyes and some new hand signal Trino didn't understand. At lunch, Trino stayed clear of the cafeteria, walking outside towards the tables where he had seen Lisana hang out.

She was there today. She sat with that girl Janie, and since it was only the two of them, Trino took a chance and headed towards the table.

Janie saw him first. "Hey, you. Heard you drew a picture of Mrs. Palacios. Naked." She nudged Lisana in the side, then laughed like a horse.

Lisana's dark eyes raised up. She wasn't laughing. Her body seemed stiff as she stared at him without speaking.

"I didn't draw any picture," Trino said. "It was Rogelio. Don't know why you'd think it was me." *Except that you're so dumb,* Trino thought.

"But he's your friend. I'm sure you both thought it was real funny," Lisana said. She sounded so cold and serious that Trino wondered if Lisana had changed into somebody else.

Trino shook his head. "Hey, Lisana, I thought it was stupid, not funny. He drew the picture on an old sheet that still had his name on it." Then he gave Janie a hard stare. "You ought to get the story straight before you start talking about it."

Janie swallowed so hard, he could almost hear all the spit sliding down her throat. She turned to Lisana and said, "Come on, let's go."

Lisana kept looking at Trino, only her mouth wasn't quite so tight around the edges. "Mrs. Palacios was very nice to me when I transferred last year. She's a good teacher too."

"She's okay," Trino said. "I like her okay."

"You shouldn't have let your friend draw that picture."

"I don't tell my friends what to do."

"Then you need some new friends," Lisana answered. She stood up from the table. "Come on, Janie, let's go to the library."

Trino didn't want her to get away. He really wanted to—needed to—talk to her more. "Maybe I could go to the library with you?" He phrased it like a question, and held his breath for her answer.

It was then Trino heard a loud whistle, a sound that he remembered when his choice had been to run or die. "Wait," he told Lisana, then slowly turned around to find out if the whistle was the same one he still heard in his nightmares.

Just on the other side of the outdoor basketball court stood Rosca and a couple of others looking towards him, just waiting and watching. Rosca's gave Trino that weird hand gesture again, then slightly jerked his head to the side to motion, *Come here.*

"What does Rosca want with you?" Lisana said.

He turned back to face her. "How do you know Rosca?"

"Who *doesn't* know him?" Lisanna said, her voice sounding disgusted. "Rosca failed seventh grade twice. Only reason he got pushed to eighth grade was because the seventh-grade teachers didn't want him back."

"He's a loser," Janie said like she knew it all. "And anyone who hangs out with him is a loser too. Right, Lisana?"

Trino could have dismissed Janie's words, but when

she wanted Lisana to agree, he could only stare at Lisana and hope she wouldn't peg him for a loser. And for some dumb reason, those words of the poem they had read together floated into his head. *I don't want to eat my birthday cake alone.*

He nearly jumped when Lisana put her hand on Trino's arm.

"Be careful of those guys, Trino," she said, looking right into his face. Her brown eyes had darkened with concern. "Rosca and his kind beat up kids and old men for kicks. I've seen him."

Trino's mouth went dry. *Me too.*

"Come on, Janie," Lisana said, and quickly walked away, leaving Janie to catch up.

He was left with no choice but to meet Rosca by the fence. The trio of boys stood slouched together, each concealing a lighted cigarette between their bodies. A quick look around, a long drag, a thin line of smoke.

"Rosca," Trino said, sliding his hands into his pockets. "*¿Que pasa?*"

"*Nada,*" he answered, and stole another slow drag off the cigarette.

Trino stood there, waiting, staring at the patches of dead grass. Then staring from his old shoes to Rosca's almost new-looking leather hi-tops; waiting for something, anything, but nothing. *Nada.* How different it was when he stood around with Lisana and her friends. Somebody usually had a story, sometimes a joke, or just a comment that made sense. He hated the silence here; it choked him. Then a low voice crawled inside Trino's head.

"Meet up tomorrow night. Car wash on Templano. Eleven-thirty," Rosca said.

Without looking up, Trino just gave one nod. Rosca tossed the burning cigarette near Trino's foot.

"Later," Rosca said, before two more cigarettes got

tossed at Trino's feet.

He didn't flinch or move, just stood where he was until the three boys walked away. One by one he ground the cigarettes into the dry grass with the toe of his shoe. The smells of worry and cigarettes, however, continued to haunt him the rest of the day.

And when he returned from school, and saw his mother there scrubbing the kitchen floor on her hands and knees, Trino had a gut feeling that his troubles had gotten worse. His mother was never home on a Friday afternoon.

"*¡Tonto!* Don't step on the floor! Can't you see I'm cleaning it?"

Trino quickly jumped onto the faded red carpet in front of the television, nearly stepping on Beto and Gus, who were watching some TV show that could barely be seen on the screen.

"And where's Felix? Didn't the bus drop him off yet?" His mother slapped a wet sponge onto the floor like she was spanking it.

"Felix probably missed the bus. He'll come home later. Why are you home so early?" He spoke cautiously, hoping he wouldn't say anything to get her madder.

His mother pressed the sponge down with both hands and pushed it across the floor. "I got fired today. That new manager—the ugly *bruja*—she said I didn't know how to do my job. Been at that stupid motel almost two years and she says I can't clean a room. Where does she think she is? At some fancy hotel? I clean up for truckers and salesmen. Not millionaires."

He understood her anger, but Trino knew the real problem was money. Even if they got a food card, there would be nothing to pay the landlord for the trailer. How he wished he was sixteen and could get a job. To be thirteen was worthless.

"I hope you ate your free lunch at school, Trino. There

isn't much to cook tonight. And I can't apply for help 'til Monday. I hope they give me a food card. They can be real mean if you say you got fired. And who'll say when I can get another job? Stupid woman. Doesn't she know I got hungry kids to feed?"

His mother cursed and complained as she continued scrubbing, but Trino stopped listening. At least she was taking her anger out on the floor, not on her kids. He only wished he had eaten some lunch instead of wandering around the school. And while he wanted just a bite of something he found in the kitchen, he didn't want to risk walking on the clean floor and have his mother start yelling at him.

So Trino just walked back to his bedroom, hoping if he got away from the kitchen, he wouldn't think of food. He flopped down on the bed, hearing the squeaky springs take his weight. He stared at the ceiling, his eyes floating over the brown water spots, warped tiles, and jagged holes made from the toy arrows that Felix got from his father last year. They spent one rainy afternoon shooting them into the ceiling.

Then he heard his mother yell his name. "Trino! Zipper and Rogelio are here!"

Trino got up and went back to the living room. He did his best to leave only one step on the kitchen floor, and pushed the screen door open towards his friends.

"What's up?" he asked Zipper, who was standing outside by the trailer kicking at the rocks.

Zipper shrugged. So did Rogelio, who stood near him.

"How come you weren't in school?" Trino asked.

"Couldn't make it, that's all." Suddenly, Zipper grabbed Trino by the shirt and pulled him away from the steps. He glanced back over his shoulder, then said in a low voice, "Did you talk to Rosca? Did he say anything important?"

Trino looked from Zipper to Rogelio. "Yeah. He wants me to meet him tomorrow night at the car wash on Templano at eleven-thirty."

"We got a job?" Zipper asked.

"We got a job?" Rogelio repeated.

Trino knew Rosca had a job in mind, maybe just breaking into the car wash machines, maybe something else. Either way, Rosca had said that Trino could get some cash.

So I can do something to help my family.

Trino realized he had made a decision to go.

Chapter Twelve
Rosca

When Trino got up on Saturday, the whole house smelled like medicine. It always meant the same thing: Beto was sick.

"You need to stay here with your brothers," his mother said, as she put Beto's empty medicine bottle into her purse. "The clinic is closed today. I'll have to take Beto to the hospital."

Trino glanced down at his little brother, who lay on the sofa. His small brown face was wet with tears, and slimy green stuff dripped from his nose. He made little honking sounds as he tried to breathe.

He sighed. If his mother went to the hospital, she could be gone all day.

And she was. She didn't return until after six. His mother was mad at the long time she had to wait. "And then the doctor wants me to buy this medicine that runs twenty dollars a bottle. I told him I lost my job and he gives me two samples. What do I do when they run out?"

Beto smelled like puke and pee. His mother took Beto, put him in her bed, then flopped down beside him to sleep too.

"Guess there won't be supper," Felix said with a shrug, and walked out of the trailer.

Trino found some peanut butter to spread on some flour *tortillas* that weren't too hard. He gave one to Gus before he ate two himself. He had been edgy all day, thinking about meeting Rosca, hoping there wouldn't be anything more than putting a crowbar into a few machines. He tried not to remember Mr. Epifaño's face or the bloody pipe that had landed near him. He tried not to hear Lisana's words in his head, *Rosca beats up kids and old men for kicks.* He kept telling himself that he had to take the job and help his mom out. What else could he do?

Since Trino no longer looked for Rosca to jump him around every corner, he took off and started walking the neighborhood. He lost track of time as he passed his school, walked around the park, and even walked to Templano Street to check out the car wash.

The car wash didn't face the busy street, but came to a V towards the corner, then fanned out, with four stalls on each side. The walls were tan brick and the trim a clean-looking blue. There was only one stall that had been spray-painted, a series of black tags from a local gang. Several stalls had people washing their cars, while another three cars were being vacuumed under the drying shed in the back. It seemed like a busy place. Why would Rosca want to meet here?

As he saw the lights on the street lamps start to flicker and shine, Trino realized he had been gone too long. His mother would probably chew him out, but at least tomorrow she could get Beto's medicine and buy some food. As he walked home, he decided he'd tell her that he found the money in the closet and that it had probably belonged to Garces. And it was theirs to keep since Garces owed them for all the food he ate.

Now that he had seen the car wash, and he had started to figure out lies to tell his mother, Trino was feeling good and confidant about the night ahead. He was even whistling as he entered the trailer park. Immediately, he saw Nick's long white car parked in front of his family's trailer. Gus was climbing on the hood with two other little boys.

Inside, Trino saw Nick sitting at the table and reading a newspaper, just like it was his house or something.

"What you doing here?" Trino asked him.

"I'm looking for you," Nick said slowly, then looked up from the paper. He wore a blue uniform shirt with a sewn-on name tag over one pocket. A round red patch on the sleeve had silver initials SMU.

Nick's black eyes passed over Trino from top to bottom before he said, "I got a job next Saturday cutting down some trees. You want to earn some money?"

"How much?" Trino said. He wasn't going to work for a few quarters.

Nick just raised an eyebrow. "Well, how hard do you work, boy? Hauling trees isn't easy. Think you could do it?"

"How much?" Trino said again.

"Could be twenty dollars if you can help me get the job finished before it gets dark." He stood up from the table and moved towards Trino.

Trino raised his chin to give the man a steady look, despite their difference in height. "How come you're asking me?"

"A boy your age needs a little cash to spend. I remember how it was."

Trino didn't comment, so Nick said, "If I don't give you a chance to earn some money, you'll find somebody to steal it from, won't you?"

Trino forced his face and eyes to remain steady, even as peanut butter suddenly rose to his throat.

His mother rushed into the room, sticking stuff in her purse and trying to comb out her tangled hair too. Her face looked very tired, yet she had plenty of energy to jump on Trino's case. "Well! You finally came back. Where you been? You just run out and leave Gus alone? Can't even find Felix. Do you know where he is?"

"No," Trino said, then swallowed back the sour taste of his crummy supper.

"You stay with Beto now while I go to Sofia's and pick up some *caldo*. It always helps Beto when he's sick like this." She looked at Nick. "Did you tell Trino he could help you next week?" Then she looked at Trino. "Nick needs you to help him. Says he'll pay you and everything."

Why should I bust my butt hauling trees? he thought.

Nick rubbed his heavy hand over Trino's shoulder. "I'll tell you more about the job later. Right now I'm going to give your mom a ride to your *tia's* house. We'll take Gus with us, but keep an eye on Beto. That *niño's* pretty sick."

Trino shook off Nick's hand and went to turn on the TV. He flopped onto the sofa as his mother and Nick went out the door. He frowned, trying to figure out what TV program was showing underneath a bunch of snowy lines shivering across the screen.

He heard the rumbles of Nick's car slowly fade away, and settled down on the sofa to wait around until he could take off. Felix finally showed up, bragging that he had eaten three hamburgers at Nacho's house, and went back into the bedroom and never came back out.

A few minutes later, Trino heard crying sounds coming from his mother's bedroom.

He'd better not puke on me, Trino thought as he slowly got up and went to check on Beto.

The little boy was tangled up in his blanket, as he whimpered and sobbed. Trino switched on a small lamp by the bed, then pulled the boy's legs free of the blankets.

Beto's wet black eyes blinked at Trino, but they seemed unable to stay focused, and then rolled back into his head before they closed again.

Trino's heartbeat sped up. "Beto? Beto, it's Trino. Are

you okay?"

He sat down on the bed, and pressed his hand on Beto's little brown arm, only to pull it away suddenly. His little brother's skin was hot with fever. Trino touched the boy's slippery forehead, then put his hand on top of Beto's chest. Each rattling breath shook over Beto's body.

Trino covered his little brother with the blanket, then went to get a wet towel from the bathroom. He had seen his mother put one on Beto's forehead before. It was all he could think of to do.

He placed the wet towel on his brother, then gently brushed Beto's damp, black hair.

"It's going to be okay, Beto. Mom'll be home soon." Trino sat down on the bed and kept talking to his brother. "Soon, you'll feel better and we can go play some video games. I'm going to get some money tonight, and I'll give you two quarters tomorrow, okay?"

It didn't take long for the towel to lose its dampness, so Trino wet it again in the sink, twisted out the extra water, and put it again on Beto's forehead. It started to bother Trino that Beto wouldn't talk back to him. He just lay there limp and wet. Trino felt raw inside.

"When I get money, you're going to get your medicine, Beto. I promise." And suddenly, Trino felt so mad that his mother was gone when Beto needed her help. Then he got madder when he thought about how she got fired from her job. He was mad that they had no money for Beto's medicine, and he was mad that somebody like Rosca was going to show him where to get some money. Why was everything getting worse and worse? By the time his mother finally got back from his *tía's* house, Trino had talked himself into a steaming anger that exploded as soon as she walked into the bedroom.

"He's burning up! Why did you take so long?" Trino got up and yelled right into his mother's worried face.

"You always have to talk and talk when you go to *Tía* Sofia's house. And Beto's so sick! Why didn't you come right back?"

She just pushed him aside, and took Trino's place on the bedside. She put her hands on Beto's puffy cheeks and slipped one hand under the towel. "All you did was put a towel on him? Why didn't you give him some medicine? Look! The bottle's right here." She reached under a pile of clothes by the bed and pulled out a skinny plastic bottle of pink pills. "He's so hot. What! You want him to die?"

Trino's own fears only intensified the anger inside him.

"I'm no doctor. I didn't know what to do!" Trino told her, tossing his hands into the air. He turned to get away only to see Nick's tall body filling the doorway. He frowned down at Trino.

"How am I supposed to find pills under her dirty clothes?" Trino yelled at Nick. "It wasn't like she had to ride the bus. She went in your junky car. How come you didn't come right back?"

"I think you need to shut up before you get into more trouble." Nick's words slid out between his teeth. He raised one eyebrow at Trino. "Yelling isn't going to help Beto."

What if Beto died and everyone blamed Trino? Such a thought only made him madder. With a surprising rise of strength, Trino shoved Nick out of the doorway and left.

"Trino, where are you going?" Nick called to him. "Come back here."

But Trino didn't answer, he only started running. Out of the trailer, out of the parking lot. Through darkened streets and alleys towards Templano Street. He had no idea of the time, but he knew a place where he could change his life. So he ran hard towards it, this change he needed so much. He cursed the barking dogs who rattled the fences he passed. He cursed the father who had died on him, and the men like Garces who called themselves *primos* but were just bloodsuckers. He cursed the destiny that made Beto sick and his family poor. He was ready now, ready to do whatever it took to change his life, the life he hated, every painful moment of it.

The night was hot and hazy as his feet carried him over sidewalks, hard ground, and uneven streets in need of repair. Few porch lights were on and many of the corner street lights had been broken out by rocks. His chest squeezed all the air out of him, but he didn't slow his steps until he could see the car wash up ahead.

Not wanting to seem overly anxious, Trino stopped by the first stall of the car wash to catch his breath. Carefully he looked around the brick wall.

He caught the shine off Zipper's vest first, and he saw Rogelio moving behind him. Then there was Rosca with his blue rag over his hair, and the two guys from yesterday's meeting.

Suddenly, three faces were like a clear color picture in Trino's hand. It was those two boys who had been with Rosca in Mr. Epifaño's that day. They had been with Rosca when Trino got jumped outside Foodmart too. And just yesterday, all three of them had thrown their cigarette butts at Trino's feet.

And now his feet felt cemented to the spot where he stood. Trino could only watch Zipper and Rosca each jam a crowbar into a different vaccum. He heard metal breaking apart and a chorus of laughter.

Out of the darkness came the first gunshot. Zipper dropped his crowbar; it clanged loudly against the asphalt. An old man in a red shirt stepped out from behind the dumpster. He cursed loudly at the boys. He gestured with a black pistol in his hand.

Rosca raised the crowbar behind him like he was swinging a bat, and lunged towards the old man. The other two followed Rosca's charge, but Zipper and Rogelio just stood there like dummies in a mall window.

Rosca yelled, the old man yelled. Another shot came. Another shot. Another.

Rosca fell, clutching his stomach, his blood spilling on the ground around him. The other two boys ran off, ran away. There was a loud scream, "No!" *Zipper's voice.*

Zipper yelled again, before he ran towards Rosca. That's when the old man aimed his pistol towards Zipper and fired again.

Zipper slumped down, fell slowly to the asphalt. Rosca still squirmed on the ground, but Zipper never moved again.

No! Trino's mouth opened, but his voice had been stolen away.

Rogelio stood by the broken vacuum, sobbing. "No, no—"

Sirens broke through the night. Red lights flashed off the car-wash walls around them.

Trino turned away from the scene, his back scraping against the wall until his bottom met the pavement. Sweat dripped down his face, but his hands and arms were too heavy to lift. He just sat there like a sack of dirty clothes. Sweat broke from every part of him. His head, his nose, even his pants were soaked. His eyes closed, blackness closing around him like a coffin.

A rough shaking brought Trino around. He opened his eyes to a strange face.

"What are you doing here, boy? Are you shot too?"

No! Trino shook his head. He had to figure out where he was, what had happened. Suddenly, everything rushed back into his mind. The guys' faces, Rosca's blood, and Zipper's last cry. *No!* His tears burned hot. "My friend is dead."

"Come on, boy. Get up," the man answered, grabbing

Trino's arm. He jerked him up to a standing position.

Trino couldn't get it together. Feeling confused, but at the same time, he remembered every detail. And the pain of what had happened and his role in tonight's events made his legs slide under him. The man jerked his body upwards before Trino hit the ground.

Suddenly, the beam of a flashlight hit Trino's eyes. He raised his hand against the intrusion, blinking at the figure in uniform.

"Good work, Joe. You caught one more," the policeman said. "Come on, boy. You're on your way to jail."

Trino found himself getting dragged towards the collection of people standing under the metal drying shed. Four or five police officers were milling around, talking to the old man. The old man's face looked sweaty as his hands gestured from the vacuums towards the bodies on the ground. One officer had put the old man's gun into a plastic bag.

Trino saw an officer handcuff Rogelio's hands behind him. Rogelio had a bad case of the shakes, still crying, "No, no, no."

Two guys with EMS emblems on the back of their shirts knelt between Zipper and Rosca, trying to check them out. One of them put a hand on Zipper, shook his head, then turned away to help work on Rosca. A taste of vomit rose in Trino's throat.

The police officer pulled Trino in front of him towards the old man with the red shirt.

"We got another one. One of the boys you said ran off," the police man said.

Now that he stared eye to eye at the man who shot Zipper, Trino spoke up in anger. "It wasn't me. I was just standing by the wall. It wasn't me, old man. Tell them."

The guy squinted, gave Trino a look over, then turned to the policeman at his side. "I don't know. The other two who ran off had baggy shirts. Like that one on the ground." He pointed towards Rosca.

Relief started to slide the edge off Trino's anger. If he got away tonight, it was because of a weird, weird luck. Beto's sickness and his mom talking too long with *Tía* Sofia had made him late. But for that, he could have been on the ground with a bullet in his gut.

"It was him," a hoarse voice called out.

Rosca lifted a bloody hand and pointed at Trino. "That's the guy who planned this job. He gave us the crowbars. Told us when to hit this place. It was Trino."

Chapter Thirteen
Flip The Switch

Trino stared down at Rosca with more hatred than he had ever felt in his life. All this time he had been silent about Rosca, saying nothing about Epifaño, telling Nick he didn't know him when Rosca jumped him at Perales. For what?

Rosca had pointed the finger at Trino. He wanted to drag Trino along to jail. Even though Trino had done nothing wrong—except for being stupid enough to think that he could trust Rosca to stay silent too.

Trino looked at the police officer who was nearest to him. "I was just standing by the wall. I didn't do anything."

"But you told me that your friend was dead." The officer who had been holding onto Trino forced him to turn around. "Did you see him get shot and then run away?"

"I was just standing by the wall." He slapped Rosca's bloody hand away from his legs. "I didn't plan any of this, man. This job was your idea, Rosca."

Rosca's voice grew louder. "Don't you say nothing, man. I know where you sleep."

If there was *un mal ojo* strong enough to kill, Trino knew it burned in his eyes. His whole face was hot with what he felt for Rosca. Never again would he let someone like Rosca run his life. Or make him run away from the truth.

"You just shut up, man," Trino told Rosca. "You got nothing on me. And if you show up where I sleep, I'll take care of what's mine. Just watch me."

"That's enough." The police officer roughly shook Trino's arm. "I just want to know about the dead boy. What's his name? Do you know him?"

Trino nodded slowly, choking back that vomit taste again. "I know him. He's my friend. Name's Zipper."

"What about that kid over there crying? Do you know him too?" the officer asked, motioning his head towards Rogelio.

Trino paused, before he said, "Yes—I know him—he's a friend too."

The police officer shook his head, then sighed. "Kid, I think you need some new friends." He released Trino's arm and moved around to question the old man further.

Trino felt forgotten as everybody wanted to talk to the old man. He said that he was the car-wash owner and told stories about all the robberies and vandalism the past few weeks. How he was just protecting his property and himself.

Moments later, Rosca was laid on a stretcher by the ambulance men. Rogelio was led away to the back seat of a police car. Two more police cars pulled into the car wash. Trino saw some boys sitting in the back seat. He couldn't tell if they were Rosca's two friends. Two policemen took the car-wash owner towards the cars. Trino guessed the man would start pointing at them too.

No one cared about Zipper, it seemed. He lay a few feet from where Trino stood. Someone had covered him with a yellow cloth.

Sorrow pressed upon Trino's entire body, making him shiver. His damp clothes clung to his skin like a layer of grease. He walked closer to Zipper's body and stared down.

It could be me. Dead. Shot. Crying in the back of a police car. Zipper, man, I'm sorry. What could I have done to save you?

○○○

Eventually, Trino ended up riding in a police car. The officer who had found Trino behind the wall said he needed to know where Trino lived. And that Trino needed to come down to the station in the morning and talk about what he had seen tonight.

Trino said nothing during the ride home, just stared at dark streets and empty places he had walked with Zipper and Rogelio. Tonight somebody had flipped the switch on all of them.

All the lights were on inside the trailer where Trino's family lived. As soon as the police car stopped outside, Trino saw Nick's tall frame fill the door, then step out from behind it.

Trino let himself out of the back seat as the police officer got out and headed for Nick.

"You Mr. Olivares?" he asked Nick.

"No. He has no father." Nick's voice carried little emotion. "His mother's inside with the other boys. Is Trino in trouble?"

Trino spoke up. "I'm okay. I didn't get arrested or nothing."

"Trino was a witness at a shooting back on Templano street. At the car wash. He knew some of the boys who broke into the machines. Can someone bring him downtown tomorrow so we can question him some more?" the policeman asked Nick.

"Nick, what is it? *Ay yi yi, la policia.*" Trino's mom had come to the door, and quickly pushed it out as she went from worried questions to a sudden anger. "Trino, where you been? What did you do? Haven't I got my hands full with Beto? Now I got to visit you in jail? How could you do this to me?"

She tried to grab Trino, but the policeman stepped between them.

"*Señora*, your son hasn't been charged with anything. We just want to question him downtown. Can you bring him to the station in the morning?"

"Downtown? *Ay*, Trino, do I got time for this?" His mom sighed loudly. "Here I am with Beto so sick, and just losing my job and—"

"Zipper's dead. He got shot at the car wash."

Her eyes widened, then she crossed herself and whispered, "*Ay, Dios mio.*"

Trino got left alone after that. The police officer drove off, and Trino's mom stayed outside talking to Nick. All Trino wanted was a dry T-shirt and his bed. It'd be empty tonight since Beto would sleep in his mother's room. Felix was asleep in his narrow bed near the closet. He didn't move or make a sound when Trino walked into the bedroom.

When Trino finally lay in the bed, thinking of everything, he wished he could just turn his brain off with a switch. He wanted to wake up and feel like his old self again. Only he couldn't stop thinking about Rogelio, who would wake up in jail. Zipper would never wake up again. Trino turned his back to the world as hot tears ran down his face and soaked into the pillow.

⊂◯⊃◯⊂◯⊃

Trino never knew when sleep finally came, but when he woke up, he felt like somebody had stomped all over him. He dragged himself off to the shower and let the hot water wash against his back and shoulders until he could somehow face the day ahead of him.

First he had to listen to *Tía* Sofia, who showed up to stay with Felix, Beto, and Gus while Trino and his mom went downtown.

"I told your mother you'd get into trouble sooner or later. Was I wrong? Huh? Huh?"

He just ignored her and waited for his mother outside. He couldn't ignore the police officer who questioned him later, though. He had to answer their questions, no matter how dumb he thought they were. Actually, Trino felt like the stupid one. He knew nothing about Rosca or his friends except that they all went to the same school. And he realized that he should know more about Zipper or Rogelio except for their last names and where they lived. He could tell the police officer honestly that the guys had only planned to meet up at the car wash; he didn't know, for sure, what was supposed to happen after that.

Trino's mother was quiet the whole time, except for a relieved sigh when the police officer told them that Trino was free to go, although he'd probably have to come forward as a witness when the case went to trial.

It wasn't until they sat together on the bus heading for home that his mother spoke to him.

"I need to know something, Trino. Just for myself. You told the police you were just standing by the wall—but— you had planned to meet them, right? Because of Beto, you were late. If not, you'd be in jail. Or maybe dead. Am I right?"

Trino turned away to look out the bus window. "Yeah."

His mother said nothing for a long while. Then she put her hand on Trino's arm.

"It's been tough for us, Trino," she said. "But I never did anything wrong to get money for my family. I scrubbed floors, washed down the neighbor's trailer, even dug holes and planted fenceposts one time. You steal from people in this *barrio* and it only makes things worse for everybody. I mean, who isn't bad off? No one can afford to lose what little they got."

Her words didn't miss their target. Trino listened, he even agreed with her. But it didn't change anything. Zipper was dead, his mother had no job, and when he got home, there would be little to eat. He still hated his life. Now he just hated it more.

Tía Sofia had some *caldo* on the stove when they got home. Trino was glad to get the hot soup inside him, but he had to listen to his aunt and his mother talk as they ate some soup too. He ate as quickly as he could, but still there was his aunt telling stories about some *primo* who went to jail and finally got the death penalty. "And he was only twenty-five!"

Trino was so glad when his uncle showed up to take *Tía* Sofia home. Trino had been sitting on the sofa, trying to press the wheels of Gus' car back onto the frame, when *Tío* Felipe came into the trailer. He was a quiet man, not very tall, with bushy gray hair.

He picked up Gus and kissed the boy on the face. He reached into his pocket and gave Gus some coins. "Save some for your brother, Beto. When he feels better, you go buy ice cream."

After he put Gus down, Trino saw *Tío* Felipe lay some dollar bills on the table. He never even looked at Trino or nothing. Just turned around and told his wife, "Let's go, Sofia."

His uncle's rejection made Trino's throat tighten up. He had always gotten along with *Tío*, but now the man wouldn't even speak to him. Things only got worse as the evening news came on their TV. Trino and Felix had been sitting on the sofa with a sniffling Beto between them. On the news there were shots of the car wash and a quick look at Zipper's body covered by the yellow cloth. There was an interview with the car-wash owner, who said, "The boys would have killed me. I had to protect myself." Even the newsman called the boys "neighborhood troublemakers," never mentioning Zipper's name. It was like Zipper didn't even matter.

"How come you weren't on TV?" Felix asked Trino.

"How come you're so stupid?" Trino responded. He got up and walked towards the door.

"Where you going?" his mom asked. She sat at the table cleaning beans and watching TV too. "I want you to stay home, Trino."

"I just want to walk outside a while."

"You'll just get yourself into more trouble. I'll turn on the TV tomorrow and see your dead body under a yellow cloth."

Her words were worse than if she had slapped him. Any thought of staying inside—trying to please his mom—suddenly disappeared He had to get away from this place where everyone thought he was just like Rosca and the others.

Trino kept walking out the screen door and slammed it behind him. He headed towards the tall tree beside the trailer, and quickly climbed up onto one of its branches, finding a spot to rest his back against the thick trunk.

He saw his mom walk out onto the step and look around for him. She glanced up and their eyes met, but she said nothing and went back inside.

He sat there as a painful jab of loneliness took him off guard. What had happened to Rogelio? Was he still with the police? Would they let him come back to school? Rogelio looked so messed up last night. Whose words would he repeat now that Zipper was gone? *Zipper, Zipper.* What was it like to be dead? Did it hurt? Was Zipper all alone? Would he be a ghost now? Or just nothing?

Trino shivered, even though it wasn't cold, and tore off a leaf to rip up. He was tearing into his third leaf when the rumbles of Nick's car caught his attention. Nick stopped his white car under the tree, and had just slammed the door when he spotted Trino sitting alone.

That's all I need. Somebody else to tell me what I did was wrong. Or just ignore me because I let him down. When's someone going to care about me? If I jumped out of this tree and broke my neck, would anyone care?

Nick looked up and spoke directly to Trino. "I want to talk to you about the job next week. And I'll get a stiff neck if I have to keep looking up into the tree. Will you come down?"

Trino sighed loudly, then took his time about climbing down. He didn't really want to take the job. Right now, he didn't want to do anything.

"Good to see you can climb a tree, Trino. I can send you up into some of the high branches I'm too big to stand on." Nick motioned Trino towards the car, and then leaned against the fender. "This lady needs a couple of Spanish oaks cut down behind her business. One's rotting away and she's afraid it will fall on her store. The other needs some serious trimming. Figured if I can get another guy to help, I can get both trees done in one day."

Trino shrugged his shoulders together, staring down at the gravel as he brushed one foot over the rocks and dirt. He couldn't think much about anything except for Zipper and Rogelio.

"Trino, are you going to help me out, or what?" Nick's voice sounded impatient.

Trino finally looked up at him. He only stared at the man. Talking just seemed to take too much out of him. He expected to see Nick get angry, but Trino got surprised. The man's eyes and mouth softened into a sympathetic expression.

"What happened last night was lousy, wasn't it?" Nick shook his head. "I'm sorry you had to see your friend get shot. It's a hard thing to watch at any age."

Trino frowned at Nick. He didn't want this man feeling sorry for him. "I'll help you cut down your trees. What time?"

Nick raised an eyebrow, then extended his hand. "I'll pay you twenty dollars for a good day's work. Let's shake on it."

Trino hesitated before he took Nick's hand. It was larger, work-rough. When they shook hands, the man's grip was firm and strong; not a painful squeeze like others made to show how *bad* they were. Trino liked the way Nick's respect made him feel.

He remembered the last thing he had told Rosca: *I'll take care of what's mine. Just watch me.* Trino looked into Nick's face as they released the handshake, and suddenly saw a good way to take care of what was his.

"Nick, any chance you could you give me the twenty dollars now? My mother needs money to buy Beto's medicine. And—and if you do this, I'll help you again. Any time."

Nick scratched his jaw as he thought about Trino's request. Inside Trino, a rumbling sense of anticipation made his legs unsteady. He had never asked a man for money this way. Was he pushing his luck?

"Actually, I could use a steady helper," Nick said. "But I'll have to try you out first. See if you can do the work."

"I can do it. Just watch me." Trino even extended his hand to Nick. "Do we have a deal? Can I get the money for my mom?"

Nick looked down, but then took Trino's hand and shook it. "I'll let you give your mother the money, Trino. I tried to give her a little money last night, but she wouldn't take it. This is a better way for everybody." He gave Trino a toothy smile that made Trino smile too.

"I like to see a boy who takes advantage of an opportunity to help *la familia*," Nick said. "But you got to take opportunities to help *yourself*, too. Not just in work, but stuff like school. So you won't just have to scrub other people's toilets for the rest of your life."

This was the second time in weeks than he had heard those words. That poet Montoya, and now, Nick. Scrubbing toilets sounded like about the worst job in the world. It's what his mother did. And Trino knew she wasn't happy with her life.

There was much to think about as Trino followed Nick inside the trailer.

Chapter Fourteen
Lisana

On Monday morning, when Ms. Juarez announced that a seventh grader named Cipriano Zepeda had been killed in an accident over the weekend, the students in Mr. Cervantes's homeroom just turned to each other with shrugs and whispered, "Who's that?"

Trino had figured no one would know it was Zipper except for the teachers. So he was a little surprised when the boy next to him looked at Trino and asked, "Is it that kid who always wears that leather vest with the zippers?"

"Yeah," Trino said in a tired voice. Up came the last image of Zipper slumping down to the ground, only to fade into a yellow body cloth.

"What happened? Do you know?"

Trino shrugged, then shook his head. The boy just shrugged too and not much else was said about "the boy who died."

As Trino went to other classes, he heard some kids in the halls talking about what had happened, even a few mentioning Zipper by name.

Coming into Coach Treviño's history class, Trino's stomach sank down to his feet. He just expected to see Zipper in the usual desk at the end of the first row, digging through his pockets for something, waiting for class to begin.

To Trino, the desk in the back seemed miles away.

"Hey, Trino. You okay?"

Trino swallowed hard before he looked behind him at Coach Treviño. The man had always been friendly, even though Trino never did much homework.

"I feel real bad about what happened to Zipper," Coach said, his big hand coming down gently on Trino's shoulder. "Were you there when he was killed?"

Trino continued to play it safe. "I just knew he got killed, that's all." He didn't offer anything else. Couldn't trust anyone not to turn words into lies and gossip.

"If you'd like, I can give you a pass to the counselor. If you want to talk. I know Zipper and you were friends," Coach told him.

"I don't need to talk to the counselor." Trino lowered his eyes and headed towards his usual desk in the back of the room. What would he say to a counselor anyway? Confess that everything was his fault? Describe when Zipper got shot? Only good thing would be that he could get out of class—but sitting some place and just thinking about Zipper wasn't appealing. He had almost been glad to get to school today, to get his mind onto something else after a Sunday that had given him way too much time to dwell on Zipper's death.

Trino sat down and made himself stare at the map that was tacked onto the wall beside him. He filled his head with names of Texas cities, rivers, and land formations—anything to keep his mind off the empty desk behind him.

Students came into the class talking and laughing about stuff like it was any other day. Then tardy bell rang and Coach Treviño rapped his knuckles loudly on the teacher's desk.

"I'm sure you all heard Ms. Juarez's announcement during homeroom period," Coach said, coming to stand close to the front desks. "Most of you probably didn't recognize the name Cipriano Zepeda. I'm sorry to tell you that it's Zipper."

Trino took his eyes off the map and looked around the room. Students stared at each other. Some faces seemed confused, some surprised, others sad. A few turned around and stared at Trino and the empty desk behind him.

"Do you know what happened, Coach?" one boy in the front asked.

Coach Treviño cleared his throat. "I was told that he was shot by accident. He was with some older boys and they tried to rob a car wash. The owner thought they were going to hurt him, so he fired his gun and it killed Zipper."

At least Coach got the facts right, Trino thought.

For Trino, history class felt weird without Zipper sitting behind him. However, walking to Mrs. Palacios' class for fourth period and not seeing Rogelio waiting by the fountain as usual, made Trino's mood slip further into a sad, dark hole.

He had stopped by Rogelio's house before school and his grandmother said that Rogelio was still in juvenile hall, and if he got out, they were going to send him to that school downtown taught by the priests. It had sounded like Rogelio was going to be in a jail forever. As Trino quietly walked into Mrs. Palacios' room, he immediately sensed something different in the students than those who had been in Coach Treviño's class.

"He was such a little jerk. No wonder somebody shot him," some girl with curly black hair said to anyone who would listen.

Some boy jeered, "Hey, Zipper. Got any bullets in your pockets?" And a bunch of kids laughed.

Trino gave that kid a dirty look, but the boy waved him off, turned to his friends and said, "You think they'll hang Zipper's vest in the trophy case by Ms. Juarez's office?"

Ignoring their stupid laughter, Trino went to his desk by the window and sat down. He felt like putting his hands around somebody's neck and squeezing away until his eyeballs popped out and a tongue that made awful jokes dangled out like a dead worm.

"All he ever did was call me roach meat," one boy said loudly. "Now he's the one who's meat for the roaches. I hope his coffin has holes. Ha!"

Trino was ready to pop up and hit him when Mrs. Palacios came into the classroom. Maybe he'd ask for a pass to the counselor, so he could get out of the room. But he was afraid Mrs. Palacios would ask a bunch of dumb questions and all the other kids would hear stuff and maybe start making jokes about him and Zipper together.

Mrs. Palacios stood in the center of her classroom and sighed. "I guess you all heard about Zipper. Seems that Rogelio got into some trouble too. I hope you will all think about what happened to these boys and learn a lesson of some kind." She turned her eyes right on Trino and said, "Some people don't get a second chance."

He just sat where he was, feeling like everyone was tearing pieces out of him. He avoided looking directly at the teacher. Even when Mrs. Palacios asked him to give the right answer on a worksheet, he said the words and kept his eyes down. When class was over, all he wanted was escape. Maybe he would drop out of school and work with Nick chopping down trees for the rest of his life.

He walked hallways filled with students, but none of them spoke to him. He couldn't shake the black mood that filled him.

Despite his mother's morning reminder to eat his free lunch because she wasn't sure there would be any food for supper, Trino didn't go to the cafeteria. Who would he sit with? Maybe kids would start talking about Zipper, or asking Trino questions.

Trino walked outside, towards the basketball courts and cement tables. He found himself a spot under a tree to sit down. He just wanted to get his head clear. He stared at the group of boys shooting hoops, laughing and running. A group of girls sat on a nearby table giggling, combing their hair, putting on lipstick and stuff. Like nothing had changed, except for what was moving around inside Trino.

No telling how long he sat there, staring and sliding between his different feelings, when he heard a girl's voice say his name.

"Hello, Trino. How's it going?"

His body stiffened slightly, before he relaxed at Lisana's appearance. When she smiled down at him, he suddenly felt—for just a few seconds—like his old self.

"Can I sit here?" she asked, pointing to a spot beside him.

"Sure, Lisana. Hi." He slid over a little so she could sit under the shade too.

Lisana sat down, then put a small denim backpack in her lap. "I was hoping I'd find you today. I've been thinking about you."

Her words made him smile a little. "Yeah?"

Her eyes lowered and she started to scratch her fingernails across her blue jeans. "I heard about Zipper—that guy was one of your friends, right?"

"Yeah, he was." Trino shifted around uncomfortably. Would she remember that Zipper had called her "pizza girl"?

"Hector said Coach Treviño looked kind of upset when he told everyone about Zipper."

"Hector?"

"My friend, Hector. He's in history class with you, remember?"

Trino shrugged, then sighed. "Sorry, I forgot. I'm—I

don't know—"

Lisana reached over and put her hand on Trino's arm. "It's okay. We don't need to talk if you don't want to. I can just sit here with you, Trino."

That's when he looked at her. Lisana was *so* nice. And here she was talking to him, just sitting with him. This all felt so much better than that lonely feeling he'd been carrying around all day. As he saw the concern in her eyes, he wondered, *Can I talk to her? Can I trust her?*

"Lisana, you ever have a friend die?"

"Sort of. My mom died two years ago." Lisana kind of smiled. "She was my friend."

Trino's hands trembled. *Her mother?* "That's too bad about your mom. How did she die?"

"A drunk driver hit her car. That's when Jimmy and I went to live with Abby." Lisana leaned back against the tree trunk, her shoulder pressing against Trino's in a comfortable way. "Poor Abby. She had just gotten married, and here come Jimmy and I to live with her and Earl. He was pretty nice about it, really. I hate to think what would happen if Abby and Earl didn't want us."

Her calm voice and close presence began to seep through that brick wall Trino had built around himself the past few days. He never expected a girl like her to be his friend.

"I haven't told this to many people, Trino. Not even Janie knows this—but my mother died on her way back from the mall. She was shopping for me and Jimmy. She died on our birthday."

Trino had never heard anything so awful. He had the craziest urge to put his arms around Lisana. What was wrong with him? He didn't even like to hug his mom, and he always pushed Beto or Gus away when they wanted something like that. Yet what she had just told him deserved more than "Gosh, I'm sorry." She had told him something that even her best friend didn't know.

He swallowed hard, then said, "Lisana, nobody at school knows this—but, I saw Zipper get shot. I was supposed to be with them—with Rosca and those guys—but I got there late. Too late, I guess."

He felt her body get stiff, then she lifted herself away from his shoulder. He was scared to look at her. He had admitted so much—maybe too much. What would she think of him?

"Ugh, Trino." Lisana ran her fingers back through her wavy hair. "I told you those guys were trouble. You're so lucky you're not the dead one. Do you realize that?" Then she sighed and shifted around to her knees so that she was looking straight at him. "Somebody told me that Rosca and the others were trying to rob a car wash. Is that what you were going to do too? Why? Tell me why?"

He didn't know how to respond to her questions. Her voice didn't sound mad, just filled with disappointment. But sometimes, there were good reasons—and her opinion of him mattered. Of all people, Lisana had to understand Trino's choice.

"I wasn't going to do it at first," he told her, trying to be as honest as he could. "But then my mom lost her job and my little brother got sick and we had no money for the medicine, so I thought that Rosca could help me get some money. I just thought we'd hit a couple of machines and take off. I didn't think some man with a gun would be there."

She just stared at him with wide-open eyes. Her face was so still, he had no idea what she thought. So he told her the rest of it—all of it. "Zipper got shot because of me. He and Rogelio never would have gotten mixed up with Rosca if it hadn't have been for me. The guys wanted a part of the job so they would be *cool*." He gave a sarcastic laugh. "I thought I could trust Rosca. I was so wrong and stupid. Now Zipper is dead, and Rogelio will have a police record. It's all my fault."

Trino stopped then, knowing he had said more to Lisana than he had told anybody. He found himself hoping that she would understand him, that she would be someone he *could* trust. He needed a friend, someone like Lisana, to care about his feelings.

Slowly, Lisana's face came back to life. Her dark eyes gleamed as she leaned her face slightly to one side. "It's not all your fault, Trino. You didn't force Zipper and Rogelio to go to the car wash with Rosca, did you? They made that choice." She gave a little sigh. "After my mom died, I blamed myself a lot. Maybe if I hadn't wanted those stupid paper plates with the purple unicorns on them for my party, maybe she wouldn't have gone to the mall that day. Once when I was crying about it, Abby reminded me that I was lucky I wasn't riding in the car with her. You were lucky too, Trino. Maybe you need to remember that when you feel sad about Zipper."

Trino shrugged his shoulders together because he didn't know what to say.

Lisana sat back on her heels. "When somebody dies, it's really awful, isn't it?"

He just nodded, only to feel sudden embarrassment as a loud noise grumbled from his stomach.

Lisanna giggled, as Trino slapped his hands onto his stomach to quiet the noise.

"I guess you're hungry, huh?" She lowered her eyes and opened up her backpack. "Boys are always hungry. Abby swears that Jimmy eats enough for three people." She rummaged through the pack and then said, "Sorry, no food in here."

"That's okay, Lisana," he said. He felt so glad to be sitting with her that even an empty stomach didn't bother him much.

"Oh—but—" Suddenly her face brightened up like a lightbulb had flipped on inside her. "Could you come over to my house on Saturday? I'm going to use that pizza coupon I won from Ms. Juarez. Abby said I could invite some friends over. You already know Hector and Jimmy. I'll probably invite Janie too. Are you busy this Saturday?"

Trino felt so excited that she wanted to include him that it took a couple of moments before he remembered his job with Nick. His earlier happiness was flushed away with disappointment.

"Aw, Lisana. I can't go. I got a job helping a man cut down trees. My family needs the money and I made a promise I'd help him." He looked into her face, hating the way her smile faded away when he gave her the bad news.

"Oh, Trino. That's too bad. But I know how it is. I have to give up stuff too if I get an extra baby-sitting job. That's how I get my money to spend." Lisana started to smile again. "I'm saving up money for a book I want from Maggie's store. She's got Jorge Morelos coming to her store in two weeks. Maggie showed me his book. It's got a black bird carrying a rosary in its beak. Have you seen it?"

Trino had to laugh. "Yeah, I have seen it. It's about some *curandero*. I read a little of it last time I was in Maggie's store." He couldn't believe it. Trino Olivares was actually talking about a book he had read.

"Oh, then, you have to come with me—when Morelos comes to The Book Basket. We both need to hear him read, Trino."

They stayed talking under the tree until the bell rang. Trino asked if maybe they could walk home together so he'd know where she lived, and she laughed and said he could.

And then Trino went back inside the school, feeling like maybe it could be a place where he belonged.